A Man Alone

Cover Artist: Eric Beetner

To Dad

1 – SUNDAY

In the end it was her crying that woke him.

Somewhere in his subconscious John Doyle heard the key in the lock, her foot upon the stair and her bedroom door open and close. But it was the soft whisper of tears that finally stirred him. He looked at the clock on his bedside table. It was 2:15. For a little while he lay there, wondering if Josie would wake and go to her daughter. She wouldn't. The vodka drunk the night before meant she would sleep till morning. Doyle sighed. He liked his beer but Josie – Josie could drink for England. Rubbing the sleep from his eyes, he sat up and listened. An alley dog barked somewhere in the distance. Another joined and their conversation roamed back and forth until a harsh voice ushered them to silence. Still he could hear her sobs permeating the thin wall between them. There was nothing else for it. Doyle blew air between his teeth and slipped from the bed.

As he moved, Josie rolled in to his space. He watched the contours of her face tighten then relax before she settled back and her breathing once again returned to normal. A cool breeze shook the blinds. Doyle shivered. He reached behind the door for the dressing gown Josie had bought him for his birthday, then padded across the landing. He paused then tapped on her door. "April." Since leaving Ireland, Doyle had cultivated a neutral tone the better to blend in. But at this early hour his voice growled with the harsh inflections of his birth. He cleared his throat and tried again. "April."

The crying stopped. Then a small, frightened voice said, "Don't come in."

April was seventeen and for the first time since he had lived there, Doyle ignored the request. He pushed open the door. Inside it was dark. Yellow streetlight strayed through the curtains creating pools of light that highlighted the photographs on the bedside table and the latest Vampire romance on the shelf in the corner. April sat in the shadow at the end of the bed. Her hands were clasped, her body stiff, and her small round face stared in surprise at his unwelcome intrusion. She tried to tell him, she tried to say she was okay, that he shouldn't have come in and should go away. But all that exited her mouth was a soul-wracking sob that burst from somewhere deep inside. She buried her face in her hands and started to cry all over again. Doyle swallowed. How small, how lost she looked and he sat on the bed beside her, put his arm around her shoulder.

It wasn't usual. Since taking up with Josie, Doyle had maintained a distance that suited them both. Their relationship was based on a respect that honored each other's privacy. They got on, Doyle would say they even liked each other, but this was different. Doyle sensed April's need. She reciprocated by burying her head in his chest. As her tears fell, Doyle rubbed her back with the flat of his hand. It was the closest they had ever been and Doyle felt a warmth, the like of which he had never known before, flood through him. As April's sobs began to subside, he held her away the better to see.

"Boyfriend trouble?"

She nodded and her blond hair fell across her face shielding it from view.

Doyle sniffed, he had seen them together once, had seen the boy hanging round the corner shops. Gerard Burns, Burnsie to his mates, a tall gangly kid with weasel eyes. Doyle didn't like him – wondered what April saw in the boy and after watching the Peter Jackson film, called him an Orc. Josie had laughed. Doyle hadn't meant it to be funny. But he knew better than to involve himself in teenage love affairs and decided to let nature take its course. He just hoped April would see the truth in the boy before too long.

"You know," he said, "things are never quite so bad in the morning." He brushed hair away from her face so he could see her eyes. Doyle's hand froze. Beneath the curve of April's cheek and against the pale smoothness of skin, a blemish, a dark stain marred the whiteness of her neck. She tried to shake her head and let her hair fall back into place, but it was too late – Doyle had seen. He placed two fingers beneath her chin and turned her head. Bruising, a series of finger-marks spotted both sides of her neck.

Doyle rose from the bed and switched on the bedside lamp. The silver stud in April's lip flashed as she turned her head from Doyle and the light. Doyle took her hands and turned them palms up. She squirmed but he held on and traced the contours of her skin with his eyes. More bruising, fingerprints stretched from wrist to elbow. Doyle felt his stomach tighten. "Did he do this?"

April didn't answer. He tugged on her hands and forced her to look at him.

April nodded.

"Did he hit you?"

April sucked in air and shook her head. "No, we were arguing and he just," she scrunched up her face as if the memory were too much, "pushed me away."

"And?" Doyle released his grip.

April shrugged and rubbed her arms. "Held me tight."

"Too tight?"

"A little."

"And put his hands around your neck?"

She wrinkled her nose. "No," she lied. "Just," she touched her throat and slipped her gaze to look at Doyle, "held me." Her tear-streaked eyes held his, wanting him to believe.

Doyle expelled a breath and squeezed her shoulder. "Okay," he said and kissed the top of her head. "Try and get some sleep."

April nodded and watched as he went to the door. "John."

He turned to look.

"Don't tell Mum."

For a moment he held her gaze then nodded. "Okay," he said, "I won't." Then he tilted his chin toward her. "You can do that in the morning."

*　　*　　*

Doyle sat at the kitchen table with a cup of black coffee in front of him. He yawned and rubbed a hand over his eyes. He hadn't slept well. The thought of *that* boy with his hands on April burned in his head like sulphur. Josie stood at the sink, washing the dirty glasses from the night before. Her hair was lank, her face drawn. She wore blue polka dot pyjamas with a white housecoat thrown over the top. Josie hadn't bothered to get dressed. Doyle looked up from his mug. She probably wouldn't bother for the rest of the day.

Back in the day, Josie MacDonald had been a real looker, a woman who had what it takes and knew that she had it. That's what people told him anyway. And in the form of her face and the arch of neck, Doyle could still see a shadow of that former self. But that was a long time ago. Yet when they met there was still something there, a vitality and impish spirit that drew him to her. They had their pasts, their histories, but it didn't matter. They drifted together like flotsam on a storm-tossed sea. But recently Josie looked tired, frayed around the edges, and the free spirit that first attracted him seemed sluggish and worn down. Perhaps they needed some excitement in their lives.

"I never heard her come in last night."

"Not surprised with what you drank." Josie's shoulders arched back as the air soured between them. Doyle added quickly, "2:15."

Still with her back to him, she nodded and rinsed a mug under the cold water.

"Don't know what she does till then."

"She's your daughter."

Josie banged the mug down on the draining board. She banged it so hard

Doyle winced. "What's that supposed to mean?"

Knowing better than argue Doyle took a mouthful of coffee. She was still staring at him when

8

April crept down the stairs. Sheepishly, she poked her head around the door and bit her lip. Josie looked at her and frowned.

"What's the matter love?"

April met Doyle's eyes and swallowed. She knew what she had to do but didn't like it, didn't like it one little bit. Doyle took it as his cue to leave. Lifting his jacket from the back of the chair, he said, "I'll get the papers."

*   *   *

Josie lived south of the city, a working class district of narrow roads and red bricked terraces. A parade of shops lined the nearby street. Among the tanning salons, burger bars and discount stores, there were plenty of shops where Doyle could have bought his newspaper. But he didn't. Instead, Doyle walked in the opposite direction. He went to Pete's, the corner shop where Burnsie and his mates hung out.

It was early and the streets were empty. Most of the houses still had their curtains drawn. Before he crossed into Cockburn Street, Doyle paused and looked over the river. It was gray and overcast, but from his elevated position he could see clear across. For a moment he paused, watching a pair of tugs shepherd a giant tanker into its berth. Turning his head, he saw something else. Dressed in black track suits, Gerard Burns and two of his cronies lounged against the shop wall eating crisps. Doyle set his jaw and walked toward them.

As he drew close, the boy nearest looked up and saw him. He nudged Burnsie with his elbow.

Burnsie narrowed his eyes. As he recognized Doyle, his shoulders stiffened. An instant later the boy relaxed, shrugged in response to a whispered warning and slinked back against the wall. He tracked Doyle until he was nearly upon them, then turned his back and placed a cigarette in his mouth. The others joined him.

Doyle waited. He heard a whisper, a giggle, but still he didn't move, surprising himself at how easy it was to slip into a role he thought long forgotten. A light was struck and the nauseous, sickly-sweet aroma of the boy's spliff drifted up from their huddle. Eventually Burnsie turned his blank face on him. Doyle stared into his weasel-slit eyes. "I want to speak to you."

"What about?"

"You know." Doyle tipped his head to the corner and away from his companions. Burnsie shrugged and followed Doyle. He cocked an eyebrow at his mates. He could handle anything the old get wanted.

He was still smiling when Doyle grabbed his neck and pushed him against the wall. The air caught in his throat and Doyle came close and kept his voice low so there would be no mistaking his words. "Leave April alone."

Burnsie couldn't move. His wide, dilated eyes stared at Doyle waiting his next move. Nothing happened. Seconds passed. Then sensing idle threats was all the man had to offer, a thin unsavoury smile spread across his lips. "Or what?" he said and his mouth twitched.

Doyle said nothing. Slowly he released his grip and stepped back. Burnsie loosened his shoulders, stood square to Doyle. He was seventeen, tall, and could stare into Doyle's face without raising his eyes. So he did. He pushed his face into Doyle's space so they were only inches apart. Doyle saw the arrogance of a boy who had walked through life doing exactly as he pleased, never once reaping the consequences of his actions.

"I do what I like when I like."

"Not with my daughter."

"Your daughter," Burnsie sneered. "Since when?"

Doyle hit him. He swept the back of his hand hard across the boy's face.

Burnsie's head spun away from the blow. His jaw sagged and his eyes widened. It was so quick, so unexpected, that he didn't react. He looked at Doyle and with trembling fingers, probed his burning cheek.

Doyle saw the other boys peer round the corner but ignored them. If they were going to jump him, they would have done so already. He stepped closer and put his index finger to the boy's throat. "I'm telling you to leave April alone. You leave her be or something bad will happen." He pushed until the boy began to choke. Then he dropped his hand and turned away. He sidestepped the boys on the corner, went into the shop.

They had disappeared by the time he left the newsagent. Doyle was calm, the brief burst of adrenaline gone as soon as he had turned his back on the boy. Others he knew retained their aggression until it found some violent or sexual outlet. But Doyle was a man who knew how to control himself. In the past it had been part of his armory, a necessity of survival, and it earned him the respect of his peers. As he stepped away from the shop, he took a deep breath and did a quick search of the street. He didn't expect any hassle but it paid to be vigilant. And that was something else he had learned in the past.

Doyle strolled across the road, unfolded the newspaper and began to read.

Engrossed in the back pages, he was passing the boarded up Beresford Arms when a black SUV swept past and pulled up at the curb. He stopped and raised his eyes. The man who stepped from the driver's side had presence – the street seemed to shrink around him. Doyle ran his eyes over him: 5'10" – stocky, faded tattoos, and biceps that bulged inside the sleeves of his white, F.C.U.K T-shirt. He had a diagonal, two-inch scar on his neck where a glass or knife had once slashed him and mean hard eyes – eyes that had Doyle square in their sights.

Moving like a beast of the mountain, he walked round the bonnet and leaned against the wheel arch. Doyle would not have been surprised to see him beat his chest with his fists. The guy took up a stance, arms folded, legs apart and eyeballed Doyle. Doyle had been in enough situations to know when trouble called. And this one was shouting at the top of its voice.

The man tipped his chin toward him. "You got a problem?"

Doyle shook his head. "None that I can think of."

The big man blew air between his teeth. It was an exaggerated exasperated action, and when he addressed Doyle, it was as if he were speaking to a stupid child. "My boys tell me you've got a beef with one of them."

"Your boys?"

He jerked his head behind him, back toward the corner shop. "They work for me. Fetch and carry, that sort of thing."

Doyle knew exactly what sort of thing.

"Young Gerard says you fronted him." He opened his hands, palms outwards in a magnanimous gesture of goodwill. "You got a problem, then you come to me and I'll sort it. Understand?"

Doyle didn't answer. He looked at the big man and started to roll the newspaper in his hand. "Not really."

The big man frowned. He wasn't used to having his word questioned. He opened his mouth then looked hard at Doyle. His head tilted to one side. "You're not from round here are you?"

"That's right. I'm not."

The big man waited and when Doyle didn't elaborate, he eased himself away from the SUV and stood in front of him. "I'm Barry Wood."

Somewhere in his head the name registered, but in truth it meant nothing. Doyle shrugged.

Barry Wood's face clouded. "Look it's like this," he said keeping his voice low and reasonable – for that's what he was, a reasonable man. "You touch one of my lads and it's like touching me. It shows a lack of respect." He opened his hands like it was a given fact, just the way of the world. And all the while he watched Doyle twirl the newspaper round and round in his hands.

Wood smiled. He prided himself on being able to see the nature of men. Some men acted hard and fronted up. But a look, the right word said in the right way, sent them crumbling to dust. A few men would never back down. Wood had met a few, the alpha males of society. Their epitaphs were written in blood across the bars and pavements of the city. But most men were weak, never looked you in the eye and allowed themselves to be walked all over. This man was one of them – an outsider he could do whatever he wanted with.

He stepped back giving the man room to think. "Now, like I said before, what's the problem?"

Doyle shook his head. The paper was now so tightly coiled that it was a rigid, cylindrical tube. "Like I said before, there is no problem."

Wood took a deep breath. The guy was an idiot. He jabbed a finger hard into Doyle's chest, so hard Doyle was forced to take a step back. "Look, dickhead. Come to me and I'll sort it. Otherwise, I'll sort you."

Doyle glanced into the big man's eyes. Nine-tenths of power lay in intimidation. Doyle knew this, had used it himself in the past. He also knew what Barry Wood didn't – that he was predictable, each word and move choreographed like a high school musical and that the element of surprise lay with him. He glanced down the street, saw Burnsie and his mates leaning against a low brick wall, watching, waiting, laughing at him like he was some soft cunt

14

from the sticks. He turned back and looked the big man right in the eye. "No, Mr. Wood," he said, "I don't think you understand." And in an underhand movement Wood never saw, Doyle jabbed the rolled up paper hard into his gut. Wood folded in the middle as the air exploded from him. Before he had a chance to recover, Doyle kicked out, bringing the flat of his heel into sharp contact with Wood's knee. As the big man's face contorted in agony, his leg buckled and he fell forward. Doyle was waiting and snap-punched him twice in the face.

And that was all.

Doyle backed away. Wood lay sprawled in the road shaking his head, wondering what the fuck happened. But it was over. Wood was in no fit state to continue the brawl. Doyle picked up his paper, brushed the dirt from the cover, and turned his back. He needed to hurry. Josie would have his breakfast on the table and it wouldn't do to be late.

*　　*　　*

But the only thing on the table was Josie's folded arms. As he walked in she glanced at the wall clock. It looked like she had been counting the minutes until he returned.

"D'you know about this?" She was smoking and ash from her cigarette fell on the table.

He acted the jerk and shrugged helplessly.

Josie stubbed her cigarette in the ashtray and tipped her chin to the stairs.

"April."

Doyle tossed the paper on the table and took a deep breath. May as well get it over with. "Yeah," he said. "I heard her come in and she told me what happened."

Josie speared him with a look. "Why didn't you wake me, why didn't you go and look for the twat?" She squirmed in the seat. "Little bastard." She pulled open a pack of cigarettes and pushed one into her mouth. Once, twice, three times she tried to light it with a cheap, plastic lighter, but a tiny spark was all it emitted. She flung the lighter across the kitchen.

"I'm not having it. Not off him or anyone." She was working herself up, bringing her anger to the boil, and God help anyone who got in her way. Doyle had seen it before, knew in normal circumstances it was best to steer clear, to go for a long walk or down to the pub until she had calmed down. She rose from the chair and thrust it back with her legs. It scraped across the floor. "I'll sort the cunt out."

Doyle grabbed her wrist. It was small and thin and his hand easily circled it.

She twisted, trying to break free and bared her teeth. Doyle suppressed a smile. He couldn't help it. When Josie MacDonald got riled, the world had better watch out. He said it was the hot blood of her forefathers bubbling through her veins. She said it was living with a shit like him. Doyle almost wished he had let her deal with Burnsie. Getting to him first had probably done the boy a favor.

He waited until she stopped struggling then held her gaze. "I've seen him. He was outside the shop and I've had a word."

16

Josie pulled at his hands. "A word, he wants more than a fucking word."

Doyle tightened his grip until she winced. "It's done. He won't bother April again."

"It's not done as far as I'm concerned."

Doyle tugged on Josie's wrist. Occasionally he had to force the point home, make sure she understood. "It ends here." Doyle stared into her eyes. The fire dimmed, and Josie took a deep breath. Reluctantly, she nodded.

"Well he'd better keep away," she said. "Or he'll have me to deal with." Doyle released his grip and she rubbed her wrist. She looked at the circle of red where Doyle had held her. "That hurt you know."

Doyle shrugged. "Sorry."

She mumbled beneath her breath and went to the sink. "Want a cuppa?"

Doyle breathed a sigh of relief. Drama over. "Tea would be good."

She turned her back. He heard water running into the kettle.

With the paper flat on the table, Doyle sat down and tried to smooth out some of the creases. He waited until the kettle began to rumble then glanced up at Josie.

"Don't know a bloke called Barry Wood, do you?"

*   *   *

Josie went ballistic. "Barry Wood," she screamed. "You've been fighting with Barry Wood?"

17

Doyle hid behind the paper. Once or twice he lifted his head thinking to stem the abuse, but it was hopeless. An overpowering silence eventually made him peer over the paper's edge.

Josie had stopped shouting and was waiting for him to speak. He didn't.

"I said what were you fighting over?"

Doyle folded the paper, laid it on the table and waited to see if she had calmed enough for him to explain. "It was the boy," he said. Josie frowned but before she could speak he waved a hand, "April's fella. After we had words, this Barry Wood got involved."

Josie's frown deepened. "Why?"

"Said that he was one of his boys. Said I should have gone to him." He shrugged, puzzled while Josie bit her lip and nodded. It made sense to her.

"That's all we need. Burnsie's in with Barry Wood's mob. Shit."

Doyle sat there waiting for her to elaborate. When she didn't, he gestured helplessly. "So, who is Barry Wood?"

"Someone you don't want to know."

"Bit late for that."

Josie took a deep breath. "He's local. Never worked in his life but owns three pubs and the bookies on Mill Street. Got something to do with Fortress Taxis too." She came forward and placed her hands on the table where Doyle was sitting. "Thing is," she said, "he's got people working for him. And not just those kids." She leaned forward to emphasize her words. "They're bad people, John."

18

Turning her back on Doyle, she began to pace the kitchen. Josie's mind went into overdrive. "Best thing," she said, "is for me to find out what's going on." She stopped and looked at Doyle. "See if he wants," she narrowed her eyes, "to see you."

Three small words but loaded with intent.

Doyle arched an eyebrow. He had made his stand and now, as far as he was concerned, it was over. "Don't worry about it Josie." He reopened the newspaper and spread it out on the table. "Everything will be fine. Besides," he said, "it wasn't really a fight."

"No?"

"I only hit him once." Doyle looked up and closed one eye, thinking. "Twice. It's just men's stuff, Josie, a misunderstanding. I'm sure Barry Wood is man enough to appreciate that."

A low hiss of air escaped Josie's mouth. "You don't know Barry Wood."

Doyle smiled. "Give it a day or two and it'll be forgotten about."

Josie looked at him and shook her head. "You don't get it do you? Barry Wood never forgets anything."

2 – MONDAY

Doyle heard the door open and bounce against the inside wall. He groaned as the sound reverberated through his thick head. He stood by the sink, wearing his dressing gown and had just poured a Resolve into a glass of water. A belch worked its way past his lips, and he waited for the hiss of salts to settle before he drank it. Josie shuffled in with the shopping, held her arms out and dropped the bags on the floor. Something split and sugar granules poured from the overturned bag. Doyle met her eyes. *Fuck. Here we go again.* Doyle turned his face to the window and gulped down his medicine. He had a throat like a bear's arse. And he figured his throbbing head was about to get a whole lot worse.

He had done the usual thing; Sunday roast then a couple of pints in the Southern Cross. But it had been a strange afternoon. He had lived there for five years, but in truth was still an outsider. And for the first time yesterday, Josie's neighbors and friends made him feel like one. The raised eyes and nods of greeting were the same as always, but there was something beneath the soft smiles and words that puzzled him.

The Cross was a mix of Reds and Bluenoses, and after Saturday's football, the place was usually alive with the piss-taking and gentle cajoling at one or the other's expense. And though there was banter and a few cracks, the laughter seemed forced. The bar was blanketed in a brooding consciousness, as if the speaker was aware that a misplaced word or action might be misconstrued and used against him.

Doyle noticed the whispers, the furtive looks in his direction. Within a few minutes, those nearest had sidled away to tables or the ends of the bar, and he found himself drinking alone. Doyle had seen it enough times in the past. The word had gone out. He was persona non grata, a pariah – and God help anyone he was seen with. It was like the old days – every conversation guarded, every bar scanned for a knife or an assassin's bullet. And it made him sick to remember. Maybe Barry Wood wasn't such a clown after all.

He left the Cross, jumped a taxi into town, and got hammered in a bar where no one knew his name. It was after midnight when he went home and crawled into bed.

Doyle turned slowly and faced Josie. She had a face like thunder. "I've just bumped into Brenda Wood," she said and pushed a hand through her hair. "Chucked her fucking trolley into me is more like." Doyle said nothing. "Brenda," said Josie confirming Doyle's guess, "is Barry Wood's wife. She pushed her fucking trolley into me at the co-op." She rubbed her ankle and flinched when she found the bruised spot.

Doyle waited, but knew exactly where this was going.

"She's not happy, *he's* not happy. Told me to tell you he's waiting to see you."

"Waiting to see me? You make it sound like a hospital appointment." Doyle frowned. Perhaps that was not a good analogy.

Josie shook her head and reached for her purse. ⬎ Inside was a business card.

"Here," she waved it in front of him, "Brenda gave me this."

Doyle took it, held it at arms length then brought it closer. Advertising Fortress Taxis, a mobile phone number was scrawled on the back. He lifted his eyes to her.

"Barry's personal number. She said if you apologize that will be it."

He looked at her and saw something he had never seen before – she was almost begging him to phone. "And you believe her?" Doyle shrugged and turned away. "It was him that started it."

"Listen to yourself." Josie's voice rose. "You sound like a kid who's had a fight in the playground." About to say more, her body sagged with the effort of arguing. She came close and rubbed his arm. "Try and understand. Barry Wood rules this place, has done since he was a kid. He's a thug, his whole family are. A brother's in Walton, his dad was killed in a shooting and his sister is doing time for drugs. As for Brenda," Josie shook her head, "I saw her outside school once, laying into a girl whose son had a fight with her Jay. And that's only her nephew. She's like a cat protecting her young that one. They're bad John, the whole family. Even Jay's on the payroll now. You really don't want the Wood family after you." She squeezed his elbow. "Make the call. Please John."

Doyle heaved a sigh and pushed the card into the pocket of his dressing gown.

"I'll think about it," he said and turned his back on Josie. He was right about one thing though; his headache had grown infinitely worse.

*   *   *

It had been a long day. Josie had gone to bed early. Doyle sat on his own in the lounge with the TV off and the room in darkness. In his hand was a glass of Jameson's. He took a sip and looked at the ceiling, up to April's room where, he presumed, she and her Facebook allies were agreeing in their assessment of him. She hadn't spoken to him. Doyle closed his eyes. A quiet life was all he wanted and in the last few years had managed to achieve a normality he once thought impossible. It wasn't perfect, but what was? He kept his head down, worked when he could, and kept himself anonymous. No fuss, no excitement – that was Doyle's way. It had to be that way.

A humorless smile creased his face. If they could see him now – Brendan Murphy, Shane Gallagher, and the others on the enforcement committee. He had been the man, the one they looked to, the man they said had ice water in his veins. What would they do now? Laugh at his predicament or put a bullet through his head? After what he had done, he guessed it would be the latter.

A crack on the window broke his thoughts. Another followed. Doyle frowned, set his whiskey down and went to the door. For a moment he stood with his ear against the wood. Outside he could hear voices, youthful and exuberant. He jerked it open and stepped out. There were four. He looked but black hoodies obscured their faces. Two were on the far side of the street, guarding their bicycles and pelting the window with stones. Arms poised to throw; they

23

froze when they saw him. The others were closer. They were by the side of the bay window, doing something to the wall. They jumped back, startled by his sudden appearance. There was a metallic clatter on the pavement and he heard a can roll into the gutter. He took a step toward them and a stone hit his chest. Covering their retreat, the boys returned to their fusillade. Doyle ducked and used his hands to shield his face. One whizzed past his head. When he looked again, they had run to their bikes and were already racing down the street. He couldn't be sure, but swore one was that kid – Burnsie.

Doyle watched the night swallow them before he went back to the hall and switched on the light. Daubed in red paint: Grass lives here.

It was the ultimate insult.

Doyle shook his head. If they knew the truth, they wouldn't call him a copper's nark. He touched the slogan. It was still wet but drying fast. If he was quick, he might be able to wash it off. Inside the house there was silence, a cocoon of false safety he knew wouldn't last.

"What was that?" Josie's tired voice called from upstairs.

"Nothing," he said. He could at least give her the night in peace. "I'll be up in a minute."

Doyle slumped back in the armchair, slugged his Jameson, and found the business card she had given him hours before. He looked at the number. Reaching for his mobile phone, Doyle made the call.

3 – TUESDAY

Doyle was at the Lisbon at 2 o'clock the following afternoon. It was the oldest and best known bar in Liverpool's gay quarter.

Against his better judgement, he'd called Barry Wood. The man wanted an apology. Doyle guessed it wasn't just an apology he was looking for. Wood suggested, the Southern Cross. Doyle said no. The Lisbon had been his idea. Wood laughed, he didn't mind. To him, one place was as good as another.

Doyle checked his watch. He had been there an hour and taken his time choosing where to sit. Occupying the basement of a Victorian tenement, little light filtered through the street level windows, leaving much of the room in shadow. He pulled a stool to the bar where he could see the door. A small glass half filled with ice and lime sat on the counter next to him. Only a few tables, those in the quieter corners and wood panelled alcoves, were occupied.

He clocked them soon as they walked in. They didn't have the demeanor of the Lisbon's usual clientele. One was squat, stocky and though younger, had the same round pug features as Barry Wood. This, Doyle guessed, would be Barry's nephew. The other man was taller with a square head that looked like it had been carved from granite. Weathered and pock-marked by some childhood disease, he looked the 'doing' type. Doyle grimaced, for he knew exactly what he was there to do.

They stopped in the doorway and swept the room with their gaze before

Square-head settled on Doyle. He bent to whisper in the other's ear and jerked his head toward Doyle. Neither looked comfortable. Doyle guessed gay bars were not on their usual agenda. He took a sip of his drink. Round one to him.

They sauntered over while Doyle ordered a refill of his Caipirinha. That Barry Wood had failed to materialize was not a huge surprise. Public place, violent encounter – perhaps he should credit the man with more intelligence.

Doyle stared straight ahead, kept his eyes on the mirror behind the bar and watched their approach. The smaller man was early twenties, wore a brown leather jacket over a hooded fleece, and almost bounced as he walked. The other wore a casual denim jacket a size too small. They closed in, one either side, hemming him into the bar. Doyle shifted. There wasn't much room for maneuvering.

Square-head leaned into Doyle's ear. "Thought we'd find you in a bar for faggots." He grinned.

"I was expecting Barry Wood," said Doyle and turned to look at the man. "I wanted him to feel at home." The grin died. Doyle saw a flicker of something in his eyes that just for a moment registered doubt.

The barman came across and placed Doyle's drink in front of him. It came with a plastic cocktail mixer to stir the Cachaca into the ice and lime.

The thug dropped his gaze to the glass, smirked, then raised it back to Doyle's face. "A faggot's drink for a faggot."

Doyle sighed and lifted the glass to his lips. The guy didn't have much of a line in offensive remarks. "Where's Barry Wood?"

"He don't waste time on scumbags like you." He gestured to his younger companion. "We're here to collect if you know what I mean."

Doyle glanced over his right shoulder. The other man was there, head tilted to one side, trying to look bad. Living in his uncle's shadow – he tried too hard.

The young barman, who had remained standing opposite Doyle, chose that moment to intervene. "Gents?" It was an invitation to buy drinks. Barry's nephew switched his gaze away from Doyle. He looked the boy up and down before his fleshy lips curled into a sneer.

"Fuck off, kid."

Doyle raised an eyebrow. Yeah, he thought. Trying much too hard.

The barman looked like he had been struck with a cattle prod. His wide eyes looked from one to the other until they settled on Square-head. Was this a joke? When Square-head snarled at him he guessed it wasn't. He raised his hands and backed off, remembering that somewhere at the back of the bar there were some shelves that needed cleaning.

Square-head grunted and returned his attention to Doyle. He laid a finger on his chest. "So this is how it's going down. Saturday at nine, you come to the Cross and apologize to Mr Wood personally. Let everyone see you do it."

"And if I don't?"

He balled his fist and cracked his knuckles. "Then you get a smack. And then another." He shook his head. "There's nothing down for you lad. One way or another, Barry *will* get his apology."

Doyle lifted the glass to his lips and sipped. The lime was sharp and hadn't fully mixed with the Brazilian liquor. He placed it back on the counter and began to stir it. "I thought Barry Wood was big enough to meet me on his own."

"Look, dickhead." Square-head was loud and the threat in his voice caused several drinkers to look around. Square-head didn't care. "Barry hasn't got time for the likes of you." He pushed his face close to Doyle's. Doyle turned his head away. The guy's breath smelled like a garbage dump. "What is it you want – a fucking hiding?"

The young barman had been watching. He had been following events, hoping they would go away. Now it was getting serious, and this was his watch, his first job, the bar entrusted to his keeping. He made a decision. Holding his palms out as they had advised on his training day, he came over to where Doyle sat. "Please gents," he said. "Take it outside." He tried to smile, diffuse the situation. He hadn't yet learned the art of looking the other way.

Square-head leaned over the counter and grabbed the kid by his shirt. He pulled him close, spat in his face. "Will you just fuck off," and he pushed him back, the force strong enough to send him sprawling to the floor. Square-head turned back to Doyle. Saliva speckled his lips. "Well. What's it gonna be?" And before Doyle said anything, added, "Remember, you got family."

Doyle stopped stirring his drink.

"A girl innit?" He leered over Doyle's shoulder and winked at his companion.

"Pretty thing, so I heard. Be a shame if something were to happen." There was a sound deep in his throat Doyle recognized as laughter.

Doyle looked at him, at his weather-beaten face, his pig eyes and didn't hesitate. He tapped the cocktail mixer on the rim of his glass then drove it straight into his face. Square-head squealed, stepped back, brought both hands to his ruined left eye. The plastic rod stuck from it like an arrow. Blood squeezed through his fingers. In the same motion Doyle brought his elbow back and cracked it into the bridge the other man's nose. Doyle felt it turn to mush. There was a muffled curse behind him.

He stepped off the stool, looked at Square-head. The pain had hit and he staggered away from Doyle, trying to understand what had just happened. "Fuck – fuck," he cursed anything and everyone. There was little danger there. Doyle turned to his right. Wood's nephew had recovered quicker than he had expected. Blood flowed from his nose over his lips and down his chin but he bared his red-stained teeth and took a wild swing. Swerving backwards, Doyle avoided the blow, grabbed the boy's outstretched wrist in his left hand and with his right caught the back of his neck. Using his weight, he turned then slammed his face into the counter. One, two, three times he beat his face into the wood then let him go. The boy slid down the front of the bar and pooled on the floor.

Square-head ripped the plastic rod from his eye and moved his head side to side trying to see Doyle through his one good eye.

"Bastard. Fucking bastard." He lurched forward, arms outstretched, trying to get his hands on Doyle. As he moved, Doyle sidestepped and struck the big man's throat with the side of his hand. Square-head choked and sank to his knees gasping for air.

Doyle looked from one to the other. They were finished, both of them. Behind the counter, the barman had raised himself from the floor and stared like he was watching a scene from a movie. Elsewhere, the commotion had caused a mini exodus. The Lisbon's customers weren't going to wait for the police. Too many questions, too many inferences in what they were doing in a *gay* bar. They grabbed jackets and briefcases and sloped out the door.

Doyle caught the eye of the boy behind the bar and held up his hands. He shrugged, thought better of saying something stupid, and headed for the exit.

It was raining. Doyle turned up his collar and crossed the road onto Mathew
Street. Soon he was lost in the crowd.

*   *   *

"So that's about it." Doyle stood by the mantelpiece, idly pushing the china figures on its top with his hand. There was a little Buddha. He picked it up and looked. The fat bastard was laughing at him. Resisting the temptation to hurl the pot-bellied twat into the hearth, Doyle carefully replaced it and faced Josie.

"That's what happened. There wasn't much I could do."

Josie sat on the couch. The lines on her forehead had deepened with every revelation until they ran like furrows in a ploughed field. Finally she buried her head in her hands.

"Christ, Jesus Christ!"

Doyle looked at the hearth until Josie managed to compose herself. "I don't believe what you're telling me." She stared at him. "I told you they're bad men, John. Men who won't take shit." She shook her head trying to think. "Who were they?"

Doyle shrugged. "I think one was Barry's nephew." Using a finger, he circled his face. "Looked similar but younger. Had thick lips."

Josie nodded. "That's Jay alright."

"The other was big, marked face and square head."

"Stonehead Duggan."

"Stonehead?" Doyle frowned then remembered the man's features. He grinned. "It figures."

"Fucking hell, John. He's a loon. You don't want him on your case." She closed her eyes and ran a hand through her hair. "You shouldn't have," she threw a hand in the air and dropped it on her thigh as she searched for the right words. "I mean you should have ..."

"Done what they wanted?" He shook his head. This was hopeless. He thought Josie would at least understand. "So you think I should have just sat there? Take what they gave out then on Saturday walk into the Cross, hold my hands

31

up and say, 'Sorry Mr Wood, it was all my fault?'"
Doyle shook his head. "Not going to happen." Josie
tried to speak but Doyle raised a hand stopping her.
"And d'you think that'd be it? D'you think Wood is
going to say, That's alright Mr Doyle. Have a drink
and let bygones be bygones? If you think that then
you're—"

"Stupider than I look?"

Doyle saw tears in her eyes. He took a deep
breath. This wasn't right, they shouldn't be fighting.
But this is what men like Barry Wood did. They drove
a wedge between people until you got so tired you
rolled over and let them do as they pleased. He
lowered his eyes. No, they shouldn't be fighting.

There was an uneasy silence before Josie spoke.

"You'll have to get it sorted."

"I can look after myself."

"It's not just you though, is it?"

"What do you mean?"

"Me and April. We live under the same roof as
you. And to a man like Barry
Wood it means we're involved."

"Well, he'll have to go through me first."

"Fucking hell, John," Josie looked at him.
"Have you heard yourself? You sound like Clint
Eastwood in a bad film." She shook her head. "I've
never seen you like this."

"We've never had a situation like this."

Josie rose from the couch and went to Doyle.
She put out a hand and touched his arm. Then she
relaxed and let her arms circle his waist. She hugged
him to her. "You're a good man, John. This just isn't
you."

Doyle pulled away from her embrace. "I've not always been."

"Been what?"

"A good man. There were times, things in the past I'm not proud of."

"When you were in the army?"

"Sort of," he said.

Her face clouded. "You've never talked about it. I thought you had a desk job. 'Force Research,' something or other."

Doyle grabbed her arm. "You forget that," he said. "Forget I ever mentioned it." He grimaced. "Christ," he said, instantly regretting that drunken night when he had let his guard down and said too much.

Josie pulled her arm free. "All right, all right." She said and rubbed her arm where Doyle's fingers had pinched. "That hurt."

Doyle held up his hands in silent apology. He was letting Wood get to him. The bastard was winning. He closed his eyes and took a deep breath.

"So what now?" she said.

"We wait."

"That's it. Just wait?"

"Not much else we can do." He shrugged. "You never know, they may find some other mug to pick on. Maybe things will blow over."

"You said that before."

Doyle turned back to the mantelpiece. Buddha's expression hadn't changed. He was still laughing at him. Doyle whistled between his teeth.

"It'll be okay," he said. But this time he was even less sure of his words.

*   *   *

Everything about Barry Wood was small time, small time operator, small time crook. That's the way he worked and that's the way he liked it. He hovered just below the police radar. And to those running the city's dirty trades – the drugs, illegals, booze and fag brigade – so long as he didn't interfere in their operations, they let him be. And he had his uses. He acted as a middleman in what he considered his part of town, ran their products to a network of distributors ready and willing to share the delights of cheap booze, Chinese cigarettes, and imported narcotics. Barry Wood was a man who knew his worth.

The Lancaster was one of his pubs. Known to locals as the Lanky, the downstairs was nothing more than a drinking den. The dark interior and low-key atmosphere was conducive to the consumption of vast quantities of alcohol. On one side of the bar, stairs led to a floor of single rooms where Barry's girls plied their trade. It was still early and business was slow. A couple of the girls lounged around the worn counter drinking cheap vodka, joining the dozen or so barflies who had only one thing on their minds, get drunk as quickly and cheaply as possible. There was little conversation. Got in the way of the drinking.

Next to the gents, and mischievously labeled Snug, was a smaller room. This was Barry's office. Flanked by Stonehead Duggan and his nephew Jay,

34

he sat at a table in the middle of the room. He ran his hand over the scar below his chin. It was a way to ↘ remember the foolishness of long ago when blind fury and a knife thrust could have ended his life. It was a touchstone, and he often used it to dissipate his anger. It wasn't working. He lifted his glass then slammed it back on the table. "This guy's taking the piss."

Stonehead fingered the patch over his left eye. Jay looked anywhere but at his uncle.

"Tell me again, what happened?"

"Took us by surprise," said Duggan, and Jay nodded, keen to agree. "Wasn't ready if you know what I mean."

Barry watched Stonehead push the tender flesh around his ruined eye. Soft fucker had discharged himself from hospital.

"Be ready next time though."

"What's that?"

Stonehead bared his teeth. "Said I'll be ready next time."

Wood nodded and pushed a brandy across the table. Duggan slugged it back.
He guessed it helped deaden the pain.

"Fast though," said Duggan.

"What's that?"

"I said he's fast. Didn't give us a chance. Sort of," Stonehead lost focus and gazed into the middle distance. Eventually he said, "Just went and did it. Unexpected like."

"That's right," said Jay. A plaster ran across the bridge of his nose and dark shadows tinged the skin beneath his eyes. "It come from nowhere. One minute we're talking and next – pow!" He threw up his hands.

Wood opened his mouth then just as quickly closed it. The boy was his sister's kid – an idiot but still his sister's kid. Sometimes he was sorry he said he'd look after him while she finished her sentence. But Brenda had insisted. And she could be very persuasive. He smiled to himself. There was nothing to her, a featherweight, but she was a mad, bad bitch, and if people thought he was a hard case, then they didn't know Brenda Wood. She kept a taser in her handbag and a .44 in her knicker draw. And if anything, *anything* happened to Jay, he'd better pack his bags and leave town. But there was something in what the lad said. He touched his cheek. It was still tender from Doyle's punch. For a little while after, he had ruminated on his actions, about what went wrong. Now Stonehead and Jay confirmed his thoughts. He had done nothing wrong. The other guy had got his retaliation in first, that's all. Wood frowned. It wouldn't have happened in the old days.

Barry was forty two. In his younger days, he had run with the Cutters and built a reputation on the terraces as a man who never took a step back, a man who fronted up whether in company or alone. From youth to man, work came easy. Firms that wanted a little extra muscle or wanted someone reliable to run the doors in town center hotspots knew who to contact. Eventually his ambitions found fruition in an extortion and protection racket that resulted in a five-year stretch in Walton.

He was smarter now and had a trio of pubs, a taxi firm, and a bookmaker's where proceeds from his various enterprises were washed through the accounts. Life was good. His drivers knew where to drop off those wanting a good time, and the girls upstairs were always grateful for the 'security' he provided. No one messed with Barry Wood. Not till now, that is. He slipped a glance at Jay. He could understand him getting a whack, kid was still wet behind the ears, but Stonehead? It was unheard of.

Something about this Doyle wasn't right. He leaned across the table. "What do we know about this bloke?"

"Doyle?" Stonehead grunted. "Just turned up five years ago and started seeing Josie MacDonald. No one knew him, or where he came from."

"He's not local?"

"Nah. Someone said he was a squaddie but…" Stonehead shrugged.

Barry Wood stroked his chin. Violence was a part of his life. These days it was enough for him to put out a word or show his face to bring people to heel. But this character, this John Doyle, either didn't know or didn't care. He took a deep breath and made a decision. Wood picked up his glass and took a mouthful – sour and flat, he pulled a face and looked at the lifeless liquid. "Jay," he handed the glass to his nephew. "Go and get the ale in."

Jay rose from his seat and as he reached for Barry's glass, saw the sly grin on his uncle's face. "What's up?"

Wood raised an eyebrow. "Tonight," he said. "I think we'll pay Mr. Doyle a visit."

* * *

The dark came early that night. Low black clouds rolled in off the Irish Sea and brought a series of squalls to the city. Hearing the rain, Doyle rose from his armchair and looked through the window. The wet streets were empty. He drew the curtains and turned back to the room. Josie was in the bath, April her room. Doyle narrowed his eyes and gazed at the ceiling. April's music thumped through the floorboards. And she *still* hadn't spoken to him.

He looked at the TV, some reality shit he had no interest in. Doyle yawned. An early night would do him good. Christ, he deserved it after a day like that. Clicking the remote, he rose from his chair then went to turn it off at the socket. The red light on the side of the TV was like a watching eye and annoyed him to hell. Somewhere in the recesses of his brain, he registered the car in the street gunning its engine.

Seconds later it was swamped by the blast of a shotgun.

Two shots in quick succession: *blam, blam*. The window imploded. Doyle dropped to the floor, hands shielding his head. Though the heavy curtain caught most of the glass, tiny slivers sped through the room. Doyle lay waiting for more – waited for the front door to be kicked down and men with guns to come bursting in. Nothing happened. Outside in the street a manic voice screamed, tires screeched on wet tarmac, and the car speeding away, faded into the distance.

A moment of silence, then Josie was shouting from the top of the stairs, "What's that – what's happening?"

38

April's door opened and a quiet, tearful voice called for mum.

Doyle crawled onto his knees and surveyed the damage. "I'm all right." He looked at the devastated window and the armchair beside it. The top had been shredded. "I'm all right," he repeated, this time to himself. Hearing Josie's step on the stairs, he shouted, "Don't come down." Instinct kicked in and keeping low, he went to the curtains. Standing to one side, he gently eased them back.

On the other side of the street, window blinds twitched as Doyle's neighbors looked out and a few doors cracked opened. But the car had gone. Behind he heard a rush of footsteps. Towel wrapped around her middle, Josie stood in the doorway.

"What the fuck?" Shock, surprise, anger, it was all there as she scanned the living room. Focusing on Doyle, her brows creased. "You're bleeding," she said and reached out a hand.

Doyle pulled back. He fingered his neck, felt the splinter of glass and pulled it free. A trickle of blood dropped onto his collar.

Josie shook her head. "What's going on?"

"Mr. Wood upping the stakes."

"This isn't a game.

"I know that. But he appears to be a man who likes to finish what he's started."

"What's happening?" Both turned to look.

April stood on the bottom stair. Her voice was small and frail. She held a bear, white with a huge red heart in its paws, close to her. Her mouth dropped when she saw the smashed window and damaged living room. She pulled the bear into her chest. "This isn't my fault."

Josie went to her. "Course it's not your fault. It's just..." She looked at Doyle, wanting him to say something, wanting him to make it better. He turned back to the window.

April pulled away. She shot Doyle a glance and her eyes narrowed. "It's him isn't it? This wouldn't have happened if he hadn't stuck his nose in."

Josie tried. "No love. It's these people." She shook her head. "John's trying to do what's right."

Doyle thought she didn't sound entirely convinced herself.

Josie put a hand out to soothe her daughter.

April shrugged it aside and stood in front of Doyle. "It's all your fault. Why did you come here? Why?" She gritted her teeth and began to scream. "I hate you John, I hate you."

Josie slapped her face.

Seconds passed. Josie's shock dissolved first and she put a hand to her mouth. "April." She reached out, wanted to hug her and tell her it was the madness going on around them. April backed away, one step at a time. Her eyes never left her mother's face. When she reached the foot of the stairs, she turned and raced away until she was out of sight. Somewhere on the landing, she burst into tears.

Doyle closed his eyes. It was Wood. Wood turning them against each other. But that was the way these things worked. He reached for his jacket and went to the door. Caught between running after April and watching Doyle, Josie grabbed his arm.

"Where the hell are you going?"

"It's best I'm not here when the police arrive."

She put her hands to her head and squeezed as if it were a way of exorcising the evil. "I don't believe this is happening?"

"It'll be okay." He opened the door and peered up and down the street.

Ignoring the stares from his neighbors, he looked at Josie. "Just you and April live here. You don't know why it happened." He stared into her eyes, making sure she understood. "A case of mistaken identity. That's all you have to say."

As he slipped through the door, Josie grabbed his hand and tried to pull him back. "I'm frightened."

He smiled and touched her face. "I'll be back before morning." Before she could say anything more, Doyle ducked his head and closed the door behind him.

*   *   *

In every city and every town, there are places where the rules don't apply. The rules that govern behavior and decency; conduct, bearing, and support for the offices of the law. These are the places where the outcasts, the dispossessed, and those living on the edge of society feel at home. To men in need, they're the first port of call. And to a man like John Doyle, it paid to know where they were.

Five years ago, alone and washed up in a city he had never before visited, he sought out those places where a man in trouble might find the things he needed. Anything could be bought for the right price, including a new identity. In the years between, Doyle kept his eyes and ears open. You just never knew.

Doyle's nose twitched as he walked through the door of the Turk's Head. An odor like something dead hung in the air. He guessed, hoped, it was from the sewers. Doyle looked at his surroundings, bare walls and peeling paint, the décor as unappealing as the punters. Already he had taken them in – the boys playing pool, the silent bar grazers, and the deal going on in the corner. For an instant they turned their heads and eyed him. Doyle knew how to behave and kept his focus on the bar ahead.

He ordered a beer. The barmaid was fifty going on eighteen: peroxide hair, gold hooped earrings, and as she turned to pour his beer, Doyle saw the lines of a spider-web tattoo stretching down from her neck and into her white vest top. She saw him looking and smiled. He bought her a drink – she liked gin, he made it a double. Said her name was Sandra. After serving one of the lads playing pool, she came round to his side of the bar and sat on a stool next to him.

Doyle took a sip of beer and looking straight ahead asked, "Know where I can buy a shooter?"

Sandra didn't flinch. She paused with the glass almost touching her lips and for a few fleeting, uncomfortable seconds, she stared at Doyle. She put the glass back on the counter. There was a hint of resignation in her voice. These days, men who bought her drink tended to want something she hadn't got.

"How much?"

Doyle shrugged. "Depends what's on offer."

Sandra nodded. "Give us a minute," she said and squeezed her hand into the pocket of her pants until she located her phone. Getting off the stool, she turned her back on Doyle and walked out of earshot. This is it, thought Doyle. She was either phoning a contact or phoning the police. She went back behind the counter a moment later. "Be in the car park at midnight," she said. "Sergei will meet you there."

Doyle raised an eyebrow. These days every East European selling dodgy gear was called Sergei. But he thanked her, bought her another gin, and moved to a table where he could see out of the window. A bitter smile played on his lips, for he remembered the way it was, every place checked for danger and an escape route should the shit hit the fan. Doyle sighed and checked his watch. Still an hour to go.

Doyle finished his beer just before midnight and went outside. He placed his glass on the counter and winked at Sandra. No police. Not yet anyway, so maybe this was the real deal. He stood beneath the porch until the car park had emptied then to advertise his presence, sat on a low wall beneath a streetlight.

It was thirty minutes later when a gray Mercedes pulled in to the car park. It turned a lazy half circle and halted fifty feet from where he sat. The driver switched his lights to full catching Doyle in its beam. Doyle winced and held up a hand to shield his eyes. A heartbeat later, the driver dipped the lights and backed in a space so that the boot faced away from the road.

Doyle took a deep breath. He had passed the first test.

There was a hollow feeling in the pit of his stomach as he walked over. Each step pulsed through him like it might be his last. But the sensations were familiar allies, and he knew from experience to trust them.

The driver watched and waited until Doyle reached the car then wound the window down. He looked at Doyle, held his eyes as if to take his measure, then opened the door. A smell of old booze and tobacco escaped the interior. "I'm Sergei," he said and held out a hand. It was big and swallowed Doyle's. He squeezed and increased the pressure until Doyle thought his bones would break. It was both greeting and warning.

Releasing Doyle's hand, he jerked his head to the to Merc's boot and walked toward it with an exaggerated swagger. He wore a black, Armani jacket, but it was scuffed and worn at the elbows, and as he bent to open the boot, Doyle saw scabbed cuts on his head. Sergei struggled. A rear end shunt had twisted the lock. He pushed and tried to turn the key but there was a knack to it. A vein throbbed at the side of his head. Cursing beneath his breath, he pushed hard and tried again. At last the barrel turned and the lid rose. He drew a handkerchief from his pocket and wiped his brow. Much like his car, Sergei had seen better days. Doyle cast him a sidelong glance. Perhaps the gun trade wasn't as lucrative as the press made out.

Sergei beckoned him with his hand. Inside were two holdalls. He pointed to the one on the left – full of handguns. Doyle prised the bag apart and began to sort through them. Even in the poor light he could see they were mostly East European, Polish Makarovs and Romanian Tokarevs. He took out a 9mm automatic and pulled back the slide. It grated, felt rough, and he tossed it to one side. Reconditioned pieces, converted blank firing pistols with mismatched ammunition waiting to explode in your hand. He shook his head and pulled a CZ 75 from the pile. A beautiful weapon but there was rust on the barrel and the lacquer was chipped. He put it back and looked at the other bag. The zip wasn't fully fastened and Doyle could see a square, black piece with a pistol grip and large magazine. He pointed. "What's this?" Sergei closed his big hand over the opening and slid the zip closed.

"Is special order."

Doyle looked back and gestured to the holdall. "This is shit."

He sensed Sergei bridle and glanced back. This was the moment when the big man might close the boot and drive away. This was the moment when he might accuse Doyle of wasting his time and go for him with fists – or something worse.

Doyle tensed and watched him pull at his lip. "You know about guns?"

"Enough."

"You soldier man?"

Doyle shrugged. "Once."

Sergei nodded. "Me too. Chechnya." He shook his head sadly. "Lost a lot of people there. Good people." He looked away and for a moment lost himself in a far off war. He heaved a great sigh and looked back at Doyle. "So what is it you want?"

"Something small and reliable, easily concealed, and accurate." He pointed a finger at Sergei. "And none of this reconditioned shit."

Sergei thought for a moment then eased Doyle to one side. Using his big hands he pushed and pulled at the contents of the holdall until he found what he was looking for. He handed it to Doyle. A revolver, a snub nosed .38. Doyle weighed it in his hand. It felt good. He swung out the cylinder and checked each chamber. Spinning it gave a satisfactory whirr. Apart from a few chips it was in good condition.

"How much?"

"Five hundred."

"Ammunition?"

He opened a compartment in the holdall and pulled out a Swan Vesta matchbox.

Inside were six shells. Doyle put them in his pocket.

"I want three reloads."

"Guns easy. Ammunition," Sergei shrugged. "Not so easy."

Doyle handed him another two hundred.

Sergei counted the money and pushed it into the inside pocket of his coat.

"You starting a war?"

Doyle shook his head. "No," he said. "But I might have to finish one.

4 - WEDNESDAY

It was the early hours of the morning when Doyle returned to the house. The taxi dropped him on the deserted main road and he walked the last mile home. He clocked the police car as he turned the corner and cut left into a side street. After a shooting, it wouldn't do to be caught with a handgun and a pocket full of bullets.

Making sure the bizzie never saw him, he backtracked and climbed the gate guarding the alley at the rear of the house. Doyle crept through the yard and went in through the back door.

Just as it clicked shut he heard Josie rushing down the stairs.

"Where the hell have you been?" She burst into the kitchen, closing her robe and trying to tie the cord before her breasts broke free of the thin material. She knotted it as if Doyle's neck was within its coil.

Doyle didn't look at her. He removed his keys and wallet from his jacket, idly patted the pocket with the .38 in it, and hung it on the back door. "I had a few things to do."

Josie tugged her hair in frustration. "For fuck's sake John. We've just had our windows blown in and you piss off out of the way."

"It's for us that I went."

She grabbed his arm and Doyle felt her desperation. "I don't understand any of this," she said. "This isn't you. And this thing with the police." She shook her head. "You've changed. You're not the man I fell in love with."

Doyle speared her with his gaze. "That's just it, Josie. I'm exactly the same man." He turned away. "Maybe you just didn't look hard enough."

She opened her mouth but before she could say any more, Doyle swept past.

"I'm going to bed," he said, then paused at the foot of the stairs. "And I suggest you do the same."

*　　*　　*

Next morning Doyle was woken by hammering and loud voices coming from the room below. Throwing on a T-shirt and jeans, he wandered down the stairs, nodding to the two workmen fitting a new window in the living room before going into the kitchen. Josie sat at the table reading some glossy magazine and didn't look up. More trouble, thought Doyle. He put a hand on the teapot, found it was still warm and poured himself a mug of tea. No use trying to push her. After five years he knew how stubborn she could be. When she was ready, Josie would say what she had to say.

But she didn't. She just sat there, drawing on a cigarette, idly turning the pages of her magazine, and saying nothing. Eventually, after what seemed an age, she lifted her eyes to Doyle, pushed her chair away from the table, and went to the drawer where the knives were kept. She pulled out the .38 and tossed it on the table. It thudded on the veneer top. Doyle looked. The barrel pointed toward him like an accusing finger. Glancing into the living room, Doyle picked up the revolver, shoved it into his waistband, and pulled his shirt over the top. Josie sat back down,

48

staring at him. He waited, then waited some more. Still, she wouldn't speak. Doyle swallowed. He could face down men in a street bar tussle or a man with a loaded gun, but a pissed off Josie MacDonald was a different prospect.

"So," he said at last, reasoning he may as well get it over with, "do you always go through my pockets?"

She slammed the table. "A gun. You've brought a gun into my house."

Doyle raised a finger and shushed her. Making sure the workmen were out of earshot, he said, "It's necessary."

"Necessary? D'you have the slightest idea what you're getting in to? And what about me and April?" She shook her head. "Who the hell do you think you are?"

Doyle's frustration spilled over and he balled his fists. "I'm just a bloke trying to do what's right, Josie. That's all. A bloke who likes a beer, who wants to come home to a family, and eat roast beef on Sundays." He looked at her and his eyes were hard as flint. "But I won't have a bastard like Barry Wood telling me what I can and can't do. I've known men like him all my life. Men who think they're king of the streets because they've cracked a few heads and got some hard cases on board." Doyle poked a finger in his chest. "Not me, not after Ireland, not after," he hesitated. "Not after what I've seen and done."

"But guns John? Where will it end?"

Doyle tipped his head toward the living room window. Hearing the row the workmen had made a discreet exit and were waiting in the van to sign off the job. "In case you haven't noticed," he said, "the use of guns has already begun."

Josie looked at Doyle like she was seeing him for the first time. For a little while she was silent. Then she sighed quietly. "You've never talked about it," she said. "Ireland, I mean. What happened?"

He ran a hand across his scalp. "I was just a kid but I should have known better. I was a soldier, and I guess I was looking for adventure, a few thrills." A harsh laugh escaped. "I got that all right." He looked Josie in the eye. "I got involved with people I shouldn't have. And when they were finished, when they'd used me up, they spat me out like a piece of filth. They gave me up Josie, gave me up and hoped I'd be 'disappeared' like others before. I ran Josie. I ran until I came here and could run no more."

Josie put a hand to her mouth. "You never said anything and we've lived together five years," she said. "I knew you were a soldier but..." Her voice trailed away. She took a breath and sat straighter in the chair. "Why *didn't* you say anything?"

"That was the whole point. If I lost myself then others might lose me too."

Josie shook herself. She stared at him as if she were in a dream and any minute might wake up. Her head ached. "This is too much," she said. "It's like the person I knew, it's like John Doyle never existed and I'm seeing you for the first time."

Doyle stared at her.

The penny dropped. "Fuck!" She ran a hand through her hair. "Your name isn't Doyle is it? What else is there? What else don't I know?"

Doyle could see tears begin to crease the corners of her eyes, but she wouldn't let them fall. Not now, not in front of him. He tried to comfort her and put his hands on her shoulders. She shrugged him away.

"So, what is it?"

Puzzled, Doyle shook his head.

"Your name?"

"John Doyle works just fine."

Josie snorted. "So it does." She got up from the chair and turned her back on him. "I'm taking April to mum's."

Doyle reached for her but she shied away.

"It's best. You can play with your guns or do what you want. But when we come back, I want things sorted." She hesitated then turned to face him. "Or I want you out."

She pushed past him. Upstairs he could hear her calling April, telling her to hurry. A few minutes later they came down, a suitcase in Josie's hand, a small holdall in April's. He met their gaze, Josie's steady and determined, April's hard and angry. She was still pissed at him.

They sat in silence until the taxi arrived. April got in first while Josie hung back. At the last moment, she wavered and looked at Doyle. "Be careful," she said and brushed his mouth with her lips.

Doyle tried to say something, to make it right. He opened his mouth, hesitated, and then it was too late. The last he saw was Josie's face behind the taxi's rain smeared window.

He went inside and closed the door.

Doyle sat in the armchair beneath the new window. His nostrils twitched, brick dust and fresh mortar reminding him of how close he had come to death. He closed his eyes and made himself breathe deep and even, bringing himself back to a level of calm. On the coffee table next to the settee, Josie had left a pack of cigarettes. Doyle hadn't smoked for years, but he took one now, finished it, and immediately lit a second. He realized how much he had missed his forty-a-day habit. He should be angry with himself for succumbing, but all he could do was relish the nicotine and deep satisfying sensation of the smoke billowing through his lungs. He came to a decision. Not one he liked, but it was the right thing to do. For Josie and April, he reasoned, it was the right thing for them.

He stubbed the cigarette in the ashtray and took out his wallet, flipped through the compartments until he found the Fortress Taxis card. For a moment he stared at the number on the back before he punched it into the phone.

It rang twice.

There was a sly bark of laughter as Wood answered and ID'd the caller.

Doyle could almost see him smirking. "We need to talk."

"Too late," said Wood. "I've always believed actions speak louder than words."

"You're frightening my family."

"Fuck your family and fuck you." Doyle heard his anger, the words forced through gritted teeth. "You should have thought about that before you fronted me."

"I did nothing but defend myself and you know that."

"You dissed me in front of my boys. And that my friend, is fatal."

"I always thought you had to earn respect?"

"Oh I've earned it all right. When I walk through these streets people call me Mr. Wood. This is my place, I was born here and they respect me for who I am and what I've done. You?" Wood sneered. "You're just some woolly-back twat who doesn't belong here, a cunt who thinks he can get away with murder. Well think again. You started this and you can take the consequences."

Doyle closed his eyes and listened to the rant of indignation, the self-styled justification, and bit down on his anger. "Look," he said and kept his voice reasonable, "we can sort this out. There's no need to involve anyone else."

"Fuck you, Doyle. I've known Josie Mac for years and what she's doing with a prick like you defies logic. If she's with you, then she's involved." Doyle felt him leer into the phone. "And when I've finished with you, I'll make sure no man looks at her again."

A chill ran through Doyle.

"You're a maggot Doyle, a worm with your belly on the ground and I'm going to tread you into that ground and make sure you never get up."

Doyle said nothing. He knew better than give Wood more ammunition. There was a pause on the line and he could almost see the man's eyes glitter, could almost see the satisfied smirk of a man who knew he had hit the mark.

He sighed into the phone. "So this is where we are."

"No," said Wood, "this is where *you* are."

"So it is Mr. Wood. Just one thing, if you try and hurt my family, I'll kill you."

Wood's laugh was a tight, sinister wheeze. "Think you're a playa, do ya?" His voice mocked him. "Good," he said, "very good." He must have pushed the phone closer to his mouth for his voice hardened and became more intimate as if this were information for Doyle and Doyle alone. "You're just one man Doyle. A man alone. What the fuck can you do to hurt me?" He let his words hang for a few seconds then spoke again. "I know where you are, so I know where to come. And I'll be coming very soon." He ended the call.

Doyle sat a little while longer then tossed his phone on to the settee. He closed his eyes and took several deep breaths. When he opened them he looked around the room. There wasn't much of him there. A battered guitar in a corner, a half read book on the sideboard. If he slipped away would anyone notice? Would it be any great loss? His eyes lighted on a photograph of Josie and April and he remembered the loneliness and despair of his life before. It wasn't an option.

Stroking the arm of the chair where he sat, a tiny sliver of glass dug into his palm. Pulling it from his skin, he watched a drop of blood form and well from the cut. Some men were relentless in their spite; cutting until they bled you dry and you were no longer able to offer any resistance. Wood was one of

54

them. And Doyle knew there was only way to deal with such men.

Rising from his chair he went to the bookcase and got down the yellow pages.

Later that day, Doyle went shopping.

*   *   *

It was midday when Doyle drove into town. He parked his Fiesta in the multi-story on Mount Pleasant and walked past the Adelphi Hotel toward the shopping center. On his way he stopped at the mobile phone store to buy six pay-as-you-go phones. From the model shop in St John's, he bought a pack of rocket igniters and motors, and at the hardware store, he bought two three-foot sections of plastic drainpipe and a dust mask. Back home, he put the materials into the backyard shed then switched on the computer in April's room. It took him ten minutes to find what he wanted on eBay. Ticking the next day delivery box, he powered down the computer and looked out of the window. Night would shroud the streets in a little more than an hour and he could continue his business. He waited, staring at the wall. This was the calm before the whirlwind he was about to unleash on Barry Wood. He needed time to clear his mind. When he was ready, Doyle put on his green fishing jacket, pulled a baseball cap low over his eyes, and pushed a pair of mini bolt cutters into his pocket. He slung an empty rucksack over his back, locked the doors, and slipped into the alley at the back of the house.

A little more than a mile from the house and backing onto a deep railway cutting, were the

Shorevale allotments. They were screened by a tangle of skeletal alders and wild vegetation. He stopped by the locked metal gates and looked back the way he had come. No one followed. Doyle jumped the railings. He skirted the path, headed toward the railway line. If anyone saw, he was just another scally taking a short-cut home.

He found what he wanted in the third shed he broke into. Since the July 7th attacks, the authorities had cracked down on the supply of fertilizers containing ammonium nitrate. But these had been lying unused for years. He stuffed two bags into his rucksack before making his way back to the house. Dumping the bags in the shed, he went upstairs and took a long soak in the bath.

That night he went back to the Turks Head. Two nights in succession – he was almost a regular. Sandra was there. Doyle gave her twenty quid and asked her to call Sergei. As she started to press the numbers on her mobile, Doyle caught her elbow and smiled. "And tell him it's for a special order."

5 - THURSDAY

Next morning, Doyle rose early. Clearing out the contents of the fridge, he brought in the supplies from the shed and smoked a cigarette. That first one always gave him a good feeling about the day. He looked at the burning end. Yeah, today was going to be a good day.

The brown UPS van delivered his parcels a little after 9. He took them to the kitchen, opened the tops, and checked the contents. In the first was one liter each of nitric and sulphuric acid. In the second, from the Perfect Pet store, a gallon of glycerine for, 'Topical use in the treatment of horses, cattle and other species.' Doyle closed and locked the doors, drew the curtains and placed the dust mask over his face. If Barry Wood wanted to raise the stakes, then he would oblige. After all, poker was his favorite game.

He broke the seals on the two bottles of acid and poured them into a glass bowl in the bottom of the fridge. He added the glycerine one drop at a time until he had a milky white solution.

Next, on a sheet of clear plastic placed on the kitchen floor, he opened the bags of Fertilizer, adding paraffin until he had a wet semi-glutinous compound. He poured the acid mix into the compound and stirred until it was evenly distributed throughout.

Doyle took a break. He smoked a cigarette on the step outside. It was years since he had done anything like this and he had forgotten how nauseous the fumes from the chemicals made him. His head throbbed, his stomach churned. Even with the windows open, the smell filled the house.

Taking advantage of being outside, he took a saw to the drainpipe and cut it into one foot sections. Back in the kitchen, he sealed one end of each pipe with black insulating tape, then carefully packed them with the mix from the floor. The motors from the model shop were filled with black powder and used to fire miniature rockets into the air. On the kitchen table, he removed the delay apparatus – a piece of cardboard – inserted an igniter, and pushed one into each tube leaving the ignition wires exposed. After programming each mobile phone, he removed the speaker and soldered the signal output to the rocket igniters. He sealed the tube using plenty of black tape and taped the phone to the outside of the tube.

At last he was finished. Six tubes containing explosive and timer lined the kitchen wall. Doyle yawned and wiped the sweat from his eyes. Time for something to eat and an early night. Tomorrow, he was going out to play.

6 – FRIDAY

Carl Maloney drove his cab into the city. It was Friday night, the kids were back at university, and the town was alive. An endless stream of taxis and buses disgorged their human cargoes into the maelstrom of the city center. Crowds hogged the bars and spilled onto pavements and roads. The town was full and split at the seams.

Friday night – best earner of the week.

Except it wasn't. Too many short trips, too many Lark Lanes and Garstons, too many 'just the end of the street please mate,' from girls showing more tit than he'd seen last year on the Costa Del Sol. Carl banged the steering wheel in frustration. His tips were shite. He stopped outside the Philharmonic Dining Rooms, peered through the windscreen and looked at his pick-up. The guy wore a green jacket, combat pants and a baseball cap. A small rucksack was at his feet and in his hand an expanding type briefcase. Carl frowned. By the looks of it, he wasn't about to break his run of bad luck.

The guy shuffled across the road and got into the back of the cab. Carl twisted his head and watched his fare settle back, briefcase on the floor, rucksack on the seat.

"Where to mate?"

He mumbled something and Carl pushed his head forward trying to hear.

"What's that?"

"Pineapple."

"On Park Road?"

"Yeah."

The Pineapple was an old coaching inn that offered rooms at reasonable rates.

Carl turned to the windscreen and put the car into gear. He guessed his tip, if he got one, would be in the reasonable bracket as well.

"Going back early tonight lad?"

"Huh?"

"I said you're going home early. Or you having a few more bevvies back at the Pineapple?" In the rear-view mirror, he saw the guy look up and caught a glimpse of his eyes.

"Maybe."

Carl detected something out of town in his accent. Maybe he should chance his arm. He pursed his lips, it was worth a try. "It's just that if you're looking for a good time, I know a place." He shrugged, "Girls, nice girls if you know what I mean."

He looked in the mirror to see if there was any reaction. "Just a thought like."

The guy was curious. "What place?"

"Not far from the Pineapple. Personal attention if you get my drift." He gave his fare a sly wink in the mirror. "I'll go in with you, make the introduction." He spoke out the side of his mouth as if he were imparting a secret. "We get a bit of commission see." What he didn't mention was instead of £50 he would be charged £70 – the difference going to Carl.

Carl thought he detected a ghost of a smile slip onto his fare's face before he shook his head.

"No. Just the Pineapple."

At the wheel Carl shrugged. "Just thought I'd ask."

Making a right, he cut along Upper Duke Street to the junction and waited for the lights to change. A steady flow of traffic headed into the city. Carl glanced at his watch. 11:30. Back in the day everyone would be going home at this time. Now things were just kicking off. The lights turned green, and he put the car into first. Sometimes he was glad he wasn't a kid anymore.

It was a straight drive, five minutes at most. Carl U-turned outside the Tesco store and pulled into a space beside the Pineapple. He checked the meter. "£3.80."

The guy fiddled in a side pocket for change and dropped coins into Carl's outstretched palm. He climbed out and slammed the door without saying a word. Carl looked in his hand. Four quid – 20p tip. "Thanks mate," he said and didn't even try to disguise his sarcasm. "I'll put it toward me new Lamborghini." He tipped the money into his wallet and drove away.

He was still smarting when he picked Shirley up outside Hannah's. She worked the bar and was one of his regulars. She folded her long legs into the back seat then pulled at her blouse trying to fan air into the opening.

Carl twisted his head and copped an eyeful. "Tough night?"

She blew. "Long, hot one."

Carl grinned. "I can see that."

Shirley saw where he was looking. "Fuck off, you old get." She tried to look demure, difficult when her skirt barely covered her arse. "Them's are for me fella's eyes," she said. "And not for the likes of you."

As she straightened herself and sat back, Carl saw her face change as she looked in the well between the seats. "Hey," she said. "Did you know there's a briefcase down here?"

*　*　*

After dropping Shirley off, Carl drove back to the Pineapple. He pushed through those standing around the bar and searched the room. The guy wasn't there. Julie was serving, and he asked her if she'd seen him. "Green jacket – baseball cap?" He used a hand to indicate his height. She shrugged, hadn't seen him nor had he taken a room, and she'd been there since six. Muttering beneath his breath, Carl threw the briefcase onto the seat beside him and drove to the office. Luckily it was just up the road.

Situated on the third floor of a retail block, its ground floor door was sandwiched between a Chinese takeaway and a florist. Carl grabbed the briefcase and bounded up the stairs. He checked his watch. This was fucking typical, shit night and now this. It was eating into his shift.

Agnes was on dispatch. She wore black - always. Tonight it was a black sweater over a knee length skirt. Her hair was pulled back tight. She was one of those women Carl thought would be more at home in some Mediterranean village, knitting and bemoaning the fate of her widowhood. He always thought there was a bit of Greek in her. Given half a chance he would like to put a bit of Irish in her too.

Sitting at her desk, telephone and radio in close proximity, she was eating a yellow cream puff. Agnes

62

narrowed her eyes, looking at Carl as he walked through the open door. It wasn't usual. Carl never went back to the office. Not even for a coffee.

Carl held the briefcase up to show her. "Some soft cunt's left this in me cab."

She shrugged in a 'what the fuck d'you want me to do about it' way and flicked out her tongue to capture a piece of cream from her top lip.

Carl put it on the table next to her. "Well has he called to say he's lost it?"

She swallowed what was in her mouth and was about to reply when a voice cut in. "What you got there then?"

Carl turned to see Billy Pierce in the kitchen doorway. He had a mug in his hand and was using a teaspoon to wring every last flavour from the teabag inside. He strolled across to Agnes, expertly flicked the teabag into a waste bin, and perched himself on her desk. Carl looked from one to the other. Billy Pierce and Aggie Watson. No wonder he got all the good fares, the airports and cross-country runs. A couple of cream puffs with a jammy doughnut would make her legs open for anyone. And he'd been trying to get there for months. Miserable bitch. He looked at her filling her face and sniffed. Anyway she had flabby tits topped with a face like a walrus. Billy Pierce was welcome to her.

Billy put his mug on the desk and lifted the briefcase by the handle. "Fuck me it's heavy." He put it back down. "Have you opened it yet?"

Carl looked at him as if he were an imbecile. "It might be something important."

63

Billy shrugged. "All the more reason to open it then." He pressed the clasp then tried again before wiping a finger beneath his nose. "It's locked."

Carl looked at him. The guy was a fucking idiot. He was going to tell him as well when the phone rang. Agnes brushed sugary residue from her fingers, shushed them with a wave of her hand before answering the call.

"Fortress cabs."

Carl watched her face change. He saw her mouth drop and eyes widen. She listened to the call and darted a glance at the briefcase sitting on the table beside her. She replaced the receiver and sat looking at the bag. Puzzled, Carl and Billy looked at each other, then at Agnes.

"Well?"

Agnes met Carl's eyes. "It was the bloke who lost that." She tipped her head toward the briefcase.

"Thank fuck for that. Tell us where he is an I'll—"

"He says there's a bomb in it."

*   *   *

Across the road, Doyle watched. A few trees grew on a small grassed area off the main road. In the dark, their spindly forms made suitable cover for a man not wanting to be seen. He had just lit his second cigarette when he saw the taxi. It was a blue Mondeo, license plate 761. It pulled up in front of the office. He watched the driver retrieve the briefcase from the passenger seat then disappear through the door of the building. Doyle checked his watch, gave him five

64

minutes, and made the call. He spoke to a woman, said what he had to, and broke the connection.

He smoked another cigarette and watched. It didn't take long. The driver along with another man emerged almost together, hesitated, then started to run along the row of shops. The woman followed them into the street a few seconds later. Wheezing badly, she stopped and started to cough. Seeing the men far ahead and fearing to be left behind, she started to jog after them. Not a good idea. Her face reddened, she began to puff, and her tits bounced as if each worked independently of the other.

There was a momentary pang of guilt as he watched her scuttle after the men.

It didn't last long. Collateral damage was always part of the deal. He took his phone from his pocket, scanned the directory. In it were six pre-entered numbers. He speed-dialed the first.

Inside the briefcase, the charge ignited. The explosion ripped through the top floor of the building, blowing the windows outwards. Fire and flame, followed by thick black smoke billowed from the open spaces. Shattered glass fell like confetti. There was a moment, a frozen moment when the world stood still – then fire and car alarms began to shriek. People were everywhere. Fleeing from the burger bars and kebab joints, they poured onto the sidewalks, spilling onto the road. Cars screeched as drivers braked hard to avoid the crowds.

Doyle watched from his position beneath the trees with a sense of quiet detachment. He nodded to himself. It couldn't have gone better. Picking up his rucksack, he walked away from the burning building.

His taxi driver had told him of a place where he could have a good time. He was going there now. Turning his head to look at the mayhem behind, Doyle smiled. But then again, he was having a very good time already.

He took his time. As he neared his destination, a small convoy of cars sped toward him. Leading was a dark SUV. Doyle pulled the bill of his cap lower until they passed. Then he quickened his pace.

Inside the Lancaster, Doyle sensed the mounting hysteria. Standing at the bar he lifted his head and could almost smell the excitement. The news of the explosion had reached the punters. It was karaoke night, but only some pissed up tart wanted to sing. Persistent as she was, the guy in charge put her off, told her next week. He was already rolling a cable round his arm, happy for once at the prospect of an early night. Doyle heard snippets of conversation, odd words as they tried to make sense of the explosion. Words like, gas, the Irish, or Muslim extremists. Why the Taliban would want to take out a taxi firm above a Chinese chippy was anyone's guess. Doyle's appearance didn't register. To them he was just another scruffy guy standing at the end of the bar.

Doyle put the rucksack on the floor, his hands on the counter. He looked round the room. The place was sparsely populated and the snug empty. Those locals who had called in for a few before heading into the city had gone. Others had followed Wood and his cronies to the site of the explosion. The Lancaster was left to those whose days and weeks tumbled one into another, whose lives were made infinitely better by the addition of alcohol to occupy the spaces left behind.

Satisfied, Doyle lifted a finger and tried to catch the barman's attention. He had a face like a fish. Turning his cod-eyed stare on Doyle and seeing he was no one of any importance, he looked away, continued his conversation. He wore a yellow T-shirt with 'Love is All Around,' printed on the front. Doyle saw the girl he was talking to. Long-limbed, athletic. She had a pretty face with long lashes and sensuous lips. But the constant demands on her body had tarnished her looks and worn her down to the point of exhaustion. She sat on a barstool, cupping her chin with a hand lest she fall asleep at the counter. 'Love is All Around?' Doyle shook his head. In this place, love was all upstairs. And had a price.

Doyle drummed his fingers on the wooden bar. He did have another way of getting the man's attention. He reached into the rucksack, his hand grasping the Mac-10's pistol grip. Bringing it into the open, he looked at it. It was small, compact, made of plastic. Apart from the barrel sticking out of the body, it didn't look like a gun at all. Doyle knocked off the safety, pushed the stock into his side, pointing at the bottles on the shelf behind the bar. He squeezed the trigger.

Three seconds. Three seconds was all it took to empty the magazine. Doyle took a step back, his eyes wide in disbelief. Now he knew why Sergei had laughed and called it "spray and pray."

The pistol grip jerked in his hand. He fought to keep the barrel down but the weapon was too light. Bullets shattered the bottles, the mirror too. Keeping his finger on the trigger, plaster from the ceiling fell around him and then it was empty. As the first shot was fired, the people in the Lancaster scattered. A table overturned, chairs fell and glasses broke. Giving Doyle a wide berth, the Lanky's customers gave no quarter in their panic to escape. They pushed one another out of the way, scrambled for the doors. It took little longer to empty the pub than it did to empty the gun's magazine.

Doyle stood in a bubble of calm. He dipped his hand into the rucksack, found the spare magazine, and replaced the empty one in the gun. Smoke wisped in the air. Doyle breathed it in, relishing the tang of an old and familiar smell. When he looked up the place was deserted. Now it was just him and the barman. He narrowed his eyes, pinning him to the spot. "Who's upstairs?"

The guy couldn't answer. Shock, thought Doyle, did that to some people.

Speaking softly he gestured with the gun. "Get the girls from upstairs – everyone from upstairs," he said. "And get them out." He glanced at his watch. "You've got two minutes."

Doyle waited. At last the guy exhaled. He hadn't taken a breath since Doyle's finger first curled around the trigger. Red in the face, thankful he wasn't on the end of another burst of gunfire, he sidled away taking the stairs two at a time. As he disappeared from view, Doyle reached for his cigarettes and lit up. So easy to get back in the habit. Then he looked at the gun's smoking barrel and his brow creased. So easy to get back in the habit.

Above him he heard doors slam, footsteps, and a babble of hard-edged foreign voices. A girl's round face peered over the banister. He waved her forward. A rag-tag line of semi-dressed girls and three crumpled men followed, one still hitching up his pants. The barman came last, treading carefully lest he annoy Doyle. Doyle cradled the Mac-10 in his arms, followed them with his gaze all the way out. He looked at his watch. Time was short. Calls would have been made, mobile phones burning hands in their desire to message Barry Wood.

Doyle took one last look, made sure the place was empty, and put the rucksack behind the bar. He tucked the machine-pistol under his jacket and strolled through the door into the night. A few people hung around outside, but no one was going to stand in his way. Once clear of the pub, Doyle walked straight and fast, crossed the road, and walked down the slope toward a line of houses. He walked until he heard the screech of tires behind then stepped away from a streetlight's glow and looked back. Barry Wood's SUV had just pulled up outside the pub.

Silhouetted against the glare of the Lancaster's frontage he watched Wood get out of his car and slam the door. Wood waved his arms, gesticulating while those left in the wake of his outrage pointed in Doyle's direction. Heads turned to look. Wood strained, peered into the gloom, and with a few men about him, started after Doyle.

Crouched down by a low wall, Doyle raised himself and levelled the Mac-10.

He fired a burst and watched Wood dive to the ground. Two others jumped a garden and took cover behind a fence. Again he squeezed the trigger. The windscreen of a parked car shattered. As far as he could tell, he never hit anyone. But hell, bullets flew everywhere. Reaching for his phone and finding 2 in his directory, Doyle pressed call.

Behind the Lancaster's wooden counter his rucksack exploded. It hammered the night and shook the houses. The sound echoed through the streets, passages, and every back alley in the district. But Doyle didn't wait to see. He was walking away – fast.

*   *   *

Doyle had left his car at the back of a scrap merchant's. It was dark and there was no one around. He tossed the Mac-10 over the wall onto a pile of loose metal – it was about all it was good for now – and drove to the Formule 1 opposite the Albert Dock. The hotel was cheap, and as its name suggested, formulaic. But it had a passing clientele that suited him. The guy at reception was foreign, disinterested, and took his money with barely a glance.

The room had just enough space to walk around the bed. Doyle disconnected the smoke alarm and lay with his head on the pillow. He smoked a cigarette, stared at the ceiling, and began to think. The house wasn't safe. Even with the place crawling with police he wouldn't put it past Wood to try something. For the moment no one knew where he was. But he couldn't stay there forever. And what about Josie and April?

His guilt was a physical thing that flushed his cheeks. Doyle hadn't thought much about them –

hadn't thought much at all. He had said this was for them, that a man like Barry Wood had to be stopped. But was it justice or a desire to return to the man he once was? And tomorrow...? Doyle took the cigarette from his mouth and blew a smoke ring toward the ceiling. He hadn't thought about that either. The man wouldn't back off, that much was certain. Wood had too much self-regard. The respect he thought was his would take a battering if he couldn't handle one man. But he would be on his guard now. Doyle would have to tread carefully. But that could wait until tomorrow. Right now he needed to sleep. He dropped his cigarette into his coffee cup and turned off the light.

Doyle heard giggles and muffled voices through the thin walls as the couple next door fucked like rabbits. Outside his window, he heard angry snarls, a shout and a glass breaking. Pleasure and pain – the twin sounds of the city. Doyle yawned and turned onto his side. He was soon fast asleep.

7 - SATURDAY

It was a black dream. Doyle was drowning. His limbs heavy, his mind numb, and every time he tried to rise from the suffocating hell, he was dragged back down. Far away a bell tolled. Was this the end? Was this…

Doyle woke with a start. The covers were wrapped around his head. On the bedside table, the stupid plastic £1 alarm clock rang fit to burst. Pulling off the crumpled sheets, he turned off the alarm and reached for his phone. Doyle switched it on, looking at the screen. A dozen, maybe more, messages from Wood detailing what he was going to do to the 'cunt' – the 'fucking cunt' that had blown away his pub. Doyle deleted them.

There was also a missed call from Josie, several in fact. When he called, she was frantic. Josie stuttered and coughed into the phone. When she had calmed enough to speak, she said just four words. And they chilled him to the bone.

"April," she said. "He's got her."

* * *

Doyle waited in his car. He had driven north of the city, to dockland – a post-industrial wasteland of warehouses and empty yards. He glanced at his watch then raised his eyes to look through the windscreen. Opposite was a box shaped building with 'Just Tires' on a sign above the door. The proprietor had left an hour before giving him a cold fish stare before rechecking the locks on the door and pulling down the metal shutters of the tire bay.

72

Whatever Doyle was doing, it was none of his business.

The conversation between Doyle and Wood had been basic: be at the Stanley dock at six and April could go free. Him for her, it was that simple. Doyle spat out the window. He doubted it would be that simple.

He checked his watch again. It was 5:40.

Doyle lit a cigarette. He knew how these things went, had been present at plenty in the past and knew the rituals, the pretense of honor, the ultimate self-sacrifice, and the clean, unfussy execution of the victim. That's the way it was when both sides knew the rules. Whether Barry Wood knew them too was another matter.

5:45. Doyle flicked the cigarette stub out of the window. The idea of driving away had crossed his mind, but April's desperate cry as Wood held the phone to her mouth before making his demands was imprinted in his head. He could as much abandon her as he could fly to the moon. Anger coursed through him. This wasn't supposed to happen. Not now, not after so many years. Doyle closed his eyes and let his anger slide. He mustn't lose it – not when he was so close.

Doyle checked the glove compartment. The .38 was there. He was tempted, but slammed the door shut. No heroics. There was one chance. It relied on Barry Wood being there and doing as he promised.

5:50. It was time. Wondering if he would get the chance to use them again, he placed the Fiesta's keys behind the sunshade and got out of the car. He walked to the T junction and turned right. On his side of the road were a string of storehouses, tired pubs, and cafés offering all-day breakfasts. On the other, gated yards of pallets and machinery. Above a gray stone wall, the arms of a giant wind turbine turned lazy circles.

The gates to the dock were locked. Doyle eased himself through a gap in the wire mesh. The outside world disappeared. His life, his being, the whole sum of his years had led to this one place and time. He looked at the water – black, viscous, seeming to pull him into its depths. The effect was disorientating and he looked away afraid of plunging into that unholy foulness never to emerge. He took a deep breath and took in his surroundings. The warehouse was longer than a football pitch and high as the water was deep. Once, ships from the empire came with their cargoes of tobacco to berth at its side. Now it was only the pigeons and rats that made use of the gray brick fortress. Doyle shivered. Above his head he saw a sign: **Trespassers Will Be Prosecuted**. Doyle's lip curled into a half smile. Abandon Hope All Ye Who Enter Here would have been more appropriate. It was that kind of place.

Steeling himself, he set off along a colonnaded walkway. It came as no surprise when, before he reached the halfway mark, they stepped from the building's shadow. Barry Wood, Jay, and Stonehead Duggan. No one moved. Doyle stared at Wood, held his gaze and searched for a semblance of humanity behind his obsidian eyes. There was nothing there.

"Where's April?"

Wood came alive. His body seemed to swell and he jabbed a finger. "Don't you say nothing." His eyes shone with glee as he appraised Doyle, a fly caught in his web. "This is my game and I make the rules." He glanced at his watch and raised his brows as if he were surprised at Doyle showing. "At least you're punctual."

Doyle clasped his hands before him like a man at prayer. It was best to say nothing. Wood paused, savoring the moment, eager to turn the screw and have his fun. But it could wait. He turned to his nephew and jerked his head in Doyle's direction. Jay pulled a semi-automatic from his jacket pocket, darted forward.

Jay trained the gun on him, pausing until Doyle held his arms out like a scarecrow. He patted him down and went through his pockets. Jay looked back at his Uncle and held up Doyle's phone.

"That it?"

Jay nodded.

Wood jerked a thumb over his shoulder and Jay tossed it into the water.

Doyle dropped his arms.

"Bit surprised," said Wood. "Thought you might try to be the hero." He shimmied like a boxer taking a stance. "Do the rescue bit." And then he smiled, a thin line of menace. "Actually, I was lookin' forward to it." He glanced back at Stonehead. "Weren't we?"

Doyle checked his watch. 6:05. "Okay," he said. "I've come as you wanted. Let me see April."

Wood held his gaze. "Why should I?"

"Because you've got what you want, because you're a man who values his reputation." Doyle focused hard on Wood. "Because if you go back on our agreement, your word will mean shit."

Doyle watched Wood's shoulders stiffen. He had hit the mark. Reputation meant everything to this guy. Wood opened his mouth then bit back his words. He swiveled his head to look at Jay then at Stonehead. Both were grinning. Then he laughed, a short bark that echoed across the water. Doyle frowned, there was something here he was missing.

"It's sad really," said Wood, "but there's something you should know." He rocked forward on the balls of his feet. "I haven't got the girl, I never had the girl. She came to us and begged me to sort it. She hates you, hates what you've done. It was her idea."

Doyle felt something inside him twist. "You're lying."

"No. Last night when we were figuring out what to do with you, my little mate, Burnsie brought her in. Said if I let her and her mam be, she'd help me get you on your own." He used a finger to trace a cross over his heart. "God's truth Doyle. It was her idea."

"I don't believe you."

Wood shrugged. "Whether you do or don't doesn't really matter. It's just a thought to take to whatever dark place you're going to. Got to say she surprised me." He shook his head. "Devious bitch. She's one to watch is that kid."

Doyle's heart beat a little faster. This wasn't going the way he planned. "So what now?"

Wood leered. "I've got you Doyle. I've got you where I want and your life's not worth a carrot. One man." He held up a finger. "That's all you were, and

76

now it's over. That's all there is to it." He walked over to Doyle, balled his fist, and punched him in the face.

A light exploded in Doyle's head. He fell back, managed to cushion the fall with his hands but still crashed hard on the ground. A foot dug into his ribs. He groaned. Blood from his split lip strayed into his mouth. He turned on his side and spat on the floor as the metallic taste registered. Doyle saw Wood standing over him, and he waited for more.

But there wasn't. Instead Wood summoned Jay.

"Take yourself off to the car."

"I want to watch."

Wood grabbed his shoulder "We're not here." He flicked a finger between them. "We were never here. Understand?"

Jay's dull eyes glimmered. If they weren't there then they couldn't be accused of anything. A slick smile creased his mouth. He stared at Doyle, grinned in a see what you've gone and done, kind of way, then turned his back and began to walk.

Doyle pushed himself to his knees. 6:10.

Wood pointed. "Don't you fucking move." He gestured Stonehead forward. In his hands was a stainless link chain. Wood looked back at Doyle. "So this is the way of it. See that?" He gestured to a metal drum lying on its side. Stonehead clipped the chain to a metal loop on its flat end. "One drum, one chain, and one stretch of water. But here's the thing. The dock's forty foot, the chain twenty." He smirked. "I won't bother to ask if you can swim."

Wood nodded at Stonehead. "Give us five minutes then do it." Once more he looked at Doyle. "Goodbye Mr. Doyle. We won't meet again."

77

Doyle watched him until he ducked beneath the gate's wire mesh and disappeared back into the living world, a world where a man's span wasn't just measured in seconds and minutes. Not once did he look back. A cold wind rippled the water, teasing the cut on Doyle's lip. He shifted his gaze to look at Duggan.

Stonehead hadn't moved. He had waited days for this moment. He made sure Doyle saw him finger his eye patch, then pulled the chain tight between his fists. A grim smile stretched across his face. Doyle tried to swallow but there was nothing there. He licked his dry lips, tasted the crust of blood that had formed and glanced at his watch. 6:13.

Stonehead watched him in silence. From his waistband, he drew a large revolver, pointed it at Doyle. It was a Brocock, a converted-gas operated air pistol. Some bright lad had discovered that by the judicious use of a drill and bit they could fire live ammunition. The underworld was awash with them. They were made from alloy, dangerous and inaccurate, but at this range Doyle wasn't taking any chances.

Stonehead tossed him the free end of the chain and gestured with the gun. "Put it round your ankle." Reaching in his pocket, he produced a large brass padlock. "Fasten it with that." He threw it to Doyle.

Doyle caught the lock. "And if I don't?"

Stonehead shrugged and extended his arm holding the gun. "Makes no difference to me". I can finish it here and now or you can have two more minutes."

Doyle checked his watch. 6:14. Every second dragged. He picked up the chain.

Stonehead laughed. "Amazing what people will do for an extra minute, an extra few seconds of existence." He sniffed the air as if it were some kind of elixir. "Makes you think how precious life is." He sat on the barrel, keeping the gun trained on Doyle, pushed the ground with his heels. The barrel moved. He snorted a laugh. "It won't be good you know." He tipped his chin in the water's direction. "Down there I mean. Fighting for breath and knowing you ain't ever going to make it." He made a mock shivering motion with his shoulders. "Me," he nodded more to himself than Doyle, "I'd take a bullet any day. Quick, simple, all done in an instant." He looked at Doyle. "I'll do you a favor if you like?" He rose from his seat, stepped forward and put the gun barrel to Doyle's forehead.

Doyle didn't move. He stared into Stonehead's good eye and waited as the cold ring of steel ate into his skull. A heartbeat passed – then Stonehead removed the gun and stepped back. He sniggered. "Nah," he said. "Too easy. I want to see you go over the side, I want... " He stopped talking and his brow creased. "Will you stop looking at your fucking watch."

6:15. Much to Doyle's surprise, the cheap, plastic £1 alarm clock kept perfect time. The blast came fifty meters from where Stonehead stood over Doyle. Not knowing exactly where the swap was to take place, Doyle had taken an early morning trip and secreted three of the bombs in various parts of the building. One had a timer in case his phone was confiscated. He figured it may be distraction enough to give him some advantage. He was right.

The explosion punched a hole in the top story of the building. Bricks, mortar, clouds of dust flew into the air. Stonehead ducked and turned to see what the hell was happening. In that instant Doyle moved. Using the end of the chain like a whip, he swung it at Stonehead.

Stonehead heard the whistle of wind too late and it caught the side of his face.

He grunted, twisted away. It was enough for Doyle. Up and running, he kicked at the hand holding the gun. There was a crack as the bone in his wrist snapped like a dry stick. The gun flew into the air. Stonehead cried out. Grasping his wrist, he tried to ease the pain, then look for Doyle. Stonehead was big and mean, but that didn't make him stupid. He knew his life depended on what he did next. He dropped his shoulder and charged, hoping to push Doyle over the edge and into the water.

Stepping to the side, Doyle cracked his fist into his face. Stonehead fell back, stumbled, and went down on one knee. He tried to rise but Doyle was on him, had picked up the chain, wrapping it around his fist, and punched him. Then punched him again and again until Stonehead's face was a bloody mess, his hand was raw, and the big man had stopped moving.

*   *   *

Twenty minutes passed and no one came. Doyle wasn't surprised. It was Saturday, the workshops and yards were closed. If anyone heard

80

the explosion, they kept it to themselves. There was football on TV and the pubs were open. Why get hassled?

Doyle sat on the overturned barrel. As day turned to night, a few security lights flickered into existence. Yellow reflections shimmied in the water like seams of gold. On the floor in front of him, Stonehead started to move. He brought a hand to his face, pawed at the dried blood and started to fold a leg beneath him. As he felt it tighten, Stonehead jerked awake. Realizing what had happened, he tugged the chain fastened around his ankle, and, hardly believing, he tugged again. Doyle got off the drum. He had retrieved Stonehead's gun and waved it as his head.

"Where's my daughter?"

Stonehead recovered. He pushed himself onto his knees, spat on the floor, and wiped his chin with the back of his hand. "Telling you nothing."

Doyle moved back to the metal drum. It was a few feet from the edge of the dock.

He tapped the side with the gun. It gave a dull clang.

Stonehead looked, followed the chain run from his leg to where it was attached to the barrel. Then he grinned. "Think I'm scared or something, think I'm a kid." He pushed his tongue round the inside of his mouth then used a finger to probe a loose tooth. Stonehead spat again. "It's true what he said you know. That girl of yours, she come to us. Barry's got her now, got something on her. And he likes 'em young. He's given her a job and everything. And d'you know what he'll do next?" Stonehead waited. Doyle didn't respond. "He'll fuck her, use her, and dump her. There won't be anything you can do about it." He began to cackle then opened his mouth and roared until the cuts on his face reopened. Blood dribbled down his chin.

Doyle put his foot on the drum. "Why should I believe you?"

"Cos it's the truth."

Doyle closed his eyes. "Just tell me where she is."

"Fuck off Doyle. You might be good with them bombs, but this is different. When you look a man in the eye, when you can smell his breath, it's not so easy." He shook his head. "Have you got the bottle?" He looked hard at Doyle, held his gaze until it seemed he knew every secret he had ever possessed. Stonehead smirked and shook his head. "Nah. I didn't think you had."

Stonehead raised himself off the ground. Stood tall and straight. Chin up, chest out, just like Barry had taught him. Doyle lowered the pistol and Stonehead laughed. He laughed even louder when Doyle turned his back. He stopped when Doyle pushed the barrel with his foot.

Stonehead's brow furrowed.

Doyle pushed harder and the barrel began to rock. Using the underside of his foot, he pushed again and it moved. It picked up momentum, rolling toward the water. The defiant glint in Stonehead's eye disappeared. His face widened into blank astonishment. "You've got to be fucking..."

There was a huge splash as the barrel went over the side. The slack in the chain disappeared, it tightened around Stonehead's ankle. As he tried to catch it in his hands and heave on the barrel's weight, his leg went from under him. He dug with his fingers, clawed at the uneven cracks in the concrete. His bloodied fingers found no purchase and he slid toward the water.

Doyle watched as the big man was swept over the side. Just for a moment Stonehead clutched the wall. He hung there, his huge strength keeping him from going down while his desperate face stared up at Doyle. Opening his mouth, Doyle thought he was going to beg for help. Then the drum dragged on the chain, Stonehead lost his grip. He slipped beneath the water with hardly a sound. Doyle walked to the edge. Nothing. The only thing to suggest Stonehead Duggan had ever existed was a series of bubbles rising from the depths. Doyle spat on the water. It was the only epitaph the bastard deserved.

He tucked Stonehead's gun into his trousers, jogged back to the Fiesta, and jumped in the driver's seat. Doyle reached for the keys behind the sunscreen, and turned the ignition. A minute later he turned it off, placed his head against the steering wheel. What Wood and Duggan had said couldn't be true. He knew April better than that. She was in danger and to save her, he had to control his emotions. So he sat there, staring through the windscreen, smoking, and thinking about his options.

How had it come to this?

Doyle closed his eyes and remembered – remembered the fear, self-loathing, the stomach churning knowledge that it wasn't right. There was nothing he could do to stop it. Even now he could see the woman's face as she opened the door and they pushed past her into the house. He remembered the screaming child in the corner. But mostly he remembered the poor bastard dropping to his knees before they emptied their pistols into his chest.

That's when he knew it was finished. His information ignored as a turf war between the army, MI5 and Special Branch, waged over paramilitary intelligence in Northern Ireland. He wanted out; they wouldn't let him, so he ran. Wanted for murder by the police, collusion by the army, and betrayal by the IRA, he ran until he found a new identity, a domestic haven in a small terraced house in the south end of Liverpool.

Now it was over.

Doyle sighed, letting out a long breath. He winced, pulled down the sunshade and looked at his lip in the mirror. There was a thin line, cracked and raw. He found some tissues to wipe his mouth in the glove compartment. Further inside was the .38. He checked the chambers and put it in his pocket. In his waistband was Stonehead's revolver. It was enough. One way or another he would find April. And if Barry Wood got in his way, so much the better. He started the car and headed back to the city. South along Wapping, into Brunswick, and over the railway to the place he had called home for nearly five years. After tonight, it would never be home again.

There were two places he reasoned where Wood might be: the Marlborough on Mill Street or the Southern Cross. Both were Barry's pubs. He would want to be seen, would want an alibi should the bloated body of John Doyle ever surface. Well, thought Doyle, he had surfaced, but not in the way Barry Wood had envisioned.

He pulled in by the Marlborough, wound his window down, and glanced across. The door of the bar was open. He could hear local duo, Dog and Bone, strangling a tune in their own inimitable style. But it was quiet. No laughter leaked from inside the bar, no smokers gathered outside the door. Another quiet night in the suburbs.

Doyle slipped the car into gear and drove to the Cross. Just before he made the left, Frank Sinatra's voice floated in through his half open window. Later it would be The Kinks, The Beatles, maybe even the Stones blasting from the boom box behind the bar. A mad Saturday's drinking had started early. The crowd huddled round the door, smoking and drinking as if there were no tomorrow. To some, the lung damaged and gray faced, perhaps there wouldn't be. Doyle didn't stop, and a little further he saw Wood's SUV at the curb. Barry Wood was partying, keeping a high profile and waiting on a call from Stonehead to say it was finished. Doyle nodded to himself. One way or another, it soon would be.

He U-turned and parked on a side street. Sank low in his seat, he waited and watched a police patrol pass. They were waving the blue flag, reassuring the residents this was a good and safe place to live. Twelve minutes later it passed again. Doyle took a deep breath, got out of the car, and walked the short distance to the Cross. He lowered his head, pulled up the hood of his fleece as he neared the bar.

Doyle paused in the doorway. Suffused with liquid laughter, a flood of voices greeted him. He scanned the room, looking for Wood. Time slowed. Adrenaline kicked in, and to his heightened senses, everyone was bigger, their movements slower, their laughter louder. Then Doyle's stomach dropped. Behind the counter serving drinks was April.

*   *   *

Barry Wood sipped his vodka-Red Bull, gazing at the people – his people. He had put a grand behind the bar knowing it wouldn't last long, but that wasn't the point. He was in the Cross, and everyone saw that he was there. From time to time, a raised glass at the bar acknowledged his presence. One or two even came over to thank and wish him well. False sentiments he knew but didn't care – he was in a mood to celebrate.

Barry glanced at the clock behind the bar. 7:15. Early as it was, the place was full. Word had spread that he was throwing his money around and the party started. Bodies jostled at the bar, urgent in their need for free beer. Music – his music, the CD Davy kept behind the bar just for him – was playing and he sat back with the self-satisfied air of a man who knows he's done a good day's work. He lifted his drink and took a large mouthful. Already he was getting a buzz, the caffeine and alcohol layering his brain in a pleasant haze. Why, he might even stick another £1000 in the till, make a real night of it.

Yeah, he was in a mood to celebrate. His chest swelled. People had crossed him before – although not like this. But doubt had never entered his mind, never once had he taken a step back. He had put

Doyle down like a mangy dog, and once again he stood on top of the pile. The grin on his face widened as he thought of Doyle going over the edge into the cold water of the dock. He had told Stonehead to film it on his phone and couldn't wait to see if the cunt begged for his life. All the sweeter if he did.

Wood frowned and checked his mobile lying on the table next to his drink.

Nothing. Dead. Nada. Wood slapped the table with his hand. What was that soft prick Stonehead doing? He had told him to text when it was finished. Knowing him he probably had a flat battery. He'd fucking kill him if he didn't have the pictures.

Wood took another drink and looked over the bar. Was Jay still flirting with Josie's kid? He had to admit that girl was really something. Her coming to him and asking to leave them alone, took a lot of bottle that. Okay, the kidnap thing was his idea and *that* was genius. But she went along and cried into the phone like a professional. If it had been the other way round, she might even have fooled him. The female of the species never failed to surprise him. He glanced across at her and shook his head. Ruthless. Never once had she asked what he was going to do to Doyle. Never once had she contemplated the consequences of her actions. Maybe the kid didn't understand the way things worked.

Wood watched her working the bar and frowned. Or maybe she did? She was a tidy piece all right. He would have to watch Jay. Start shagging that and he might get ideas. Wood grinned. Jay was a good kid but green. A good fuck might do him good.

Wood laughed, and rubbed his chin. A good fuck would do him good too.

Barry Wood raised his head, straining his neck over those around him so he could look a little closer at the girl. He wasn't alone in his appraisal of April MacDonald. There was a guy standing at the back of the bar scrum who had an equal interest. He picked up his glass and froze with it half way to his lips. "Fuck me." A hand clenched his guts. It couldn't be. He tried to shout a warning to Jay, but he was slow. His voice caught, and he looked across at his nephew with a growing sense of dread.

But Jay had already seen, was reaching inside his pocket for the gun he carried. Wood looked again at the stranger, narrowing his eyes the better to see his face. It was the face of a ghost. John Doyle had come back to haunt him.

*　　*　　*

April didn't have time to think. She took two empty glasses off the counter and looked at the face behind them. "Lager and a brown mixed." She nodded and turned to the fridge for a bottle of Mann's. Using a sleeve, she wiped sweat from her eyes. Harassed and busy, why the fuck had she asked Barry for a job?

She looked across to where he was sitting, could hardly believe what she had done. Everyone knew he was a bad man. But mum had brought her up to be frightened of no one. So she did what she had to and put it on the line. Said she would do what he wanted so long as they left mum and her alone.

And Barry had liked that, liked the fact she stared him in the eye and didn't flinch. April smiled, remembered the look he had given her. The smile turned into a frown. What about John? She bit her lip. The truth was she hadn't thought about him. But why should she? Who the fuck did he think he was anyway, Jason Bourne? There was a momentary flash of something April dimly recognized as guilt. It quickly evaporated. Something else her mum once said – family before all. And mum was the only family she had.

"April!" Davy Carpenter called her from the end of the bar he was working. He lifted his chin in a 'what's up' kind of way. She waved a hand. Distracted was all.

April handed the beers across the counter. The guy slipped her a 20p tip.

She tossed it into the glass by the side of the till and wondered how long Barry's money would last. Not long when everyone knew there was free beer. She glanced over at Davy Carpenter. He was working like a dog and for what? Minimum wage and a drink from Barry. And when was the last time he took a grand in a night? Two hours into her shift she realized bar work wasn't for her. Even as she said it an idea seeped into her mind. No, bar work wasn't for her, but she could run one, run it better than Davy Carpenter. Her mood lightened. Perhaps she could run one for Barry?

A quiver of excitement passed through her. If she did well tonight she might put it to him. She had ideas. Live music and food – hot food. A pan of scouse or a chilli would keep the punters interested. Yeah she might put it to him later.

She took another glass and held it beneath the lager pump. Brushing her fringe out of her eyes, she gazed at the faces cluttered around the bar. Just for a second, the bodies parted. Staring straight at her was John. His lip was swollen and a black mark showed on his cheek. April's eyes widened. Lager flowed over her hand and into the tray. She couldn't speak, couldn't move. And John just stood there and stared and stared into her face. She tried to smile, tried to make things right. But just before the sea of faces closed in and John's face was lost from view, she looked into his eyes and saw something she had never before seen. He knew, she swore that he knew.

The glass of lager slipped from her fingers.

*   *   *

Doyle was aware of a hollow in his stomach. A growing emptiness that spread to every part of his body. He thought he understood people, thought he knew April and Josie at least. Five years and turned out he knew fuck all. He watched the glass fall from April's hand until it shattered on the floor. It broke the spell. A few light-hearted cheers and laughs followed. But Doyle wasn't listening. His neck began to tingle. The sixth-sense itch of self-preservation had kicked in and as he turned, his eyes locked on Jay. He had that same stupid look on his face Doyle had first seen in the Lisbon. He watched Jay trying to pull a pistol, a Beretta. It was a beautiful piece, black lacquered, clean, and never fired in anger. But it was

90

caught on the lining of his pocket and he cursed, trying to drag it clear. Pulling harder, the material ripped and as his finger snagged the trigger, the gun went off.

The blast reverberated through the room. There was a collective gasp as people ducked and pulled in their necks. A girl screamed. Others raised their heads searching for the source of the explosion. Someone recognized Doyle and swore. "Fuckin' hell!"

And as they looked and saw, they couldn't believe that John Doyle was fool enough to step into the heart of Barry Wood's empire. A girl's voice cut through the silence, "Oh – my – God!" And a whirr of movement followed. Faces blurred as they hurried out of the way to make circles of open space around Doyle, Jay, and Barry Wood. They moved to the edges of the room. A pause as breaths were held waiting the next move. One man sidled through the door, others ran, and they deserted the Southern Cross as if they had never been there at all.

Doyle stared at Jay as the room emptied around them.

"Christ – Jesus Christ." He was jumping around, hopping and screaming in agony.

There was a hole in one of his new trainers. Asics Kayano's, a hundred and twenty nine quid from Foot Locker. Blood began to stain the side.

Jay bit his lip and stifled another scream. He shouldn't have left one in the chamber. Someone should have told him not to leave one in the chamber. He turned, looking for his uncle, the man who always knew what to do.

Barry hadn't moved. Leaning over the table he was waving his arms. "Jay," he shouted. "The gun. Use the fucking gun."

Jay looked at it as if it had magically appeared in his hand then remembered why it was there. Forgetting his pain, he raised the Beretta and pointed it at Doyle.

Doyle didn't give him a chance. He pulled the Brocock from his belt, drew a bead on Jay and fired twice. The first bullet hit him in the face. It must have passed straight through for as he fell back, a spray of blood and brain splattered the wall behind. The second blew the gun apart. Doyle cursed – blamed himself for using the cheap shit and not the .38. He looked at his hand. Messy and blood streaked – he was sure he had lost a finger. Behind the counter, April screamed.

Doyle clasped his right hand within his left and surveyed the damage. Not as bad as he first feared, but the tips of his middle and index fingers were shredded. He gritted his teeth, sucking in air as the pain started. But things were about to get a whole lot worse.

Barry crawled to his nephew. Jay lay on his back. A third eye had opened in the middle of his forehead and dark blood pooled about him. Taking Jay's gun from the floor, he rose from a crouch and pointed it at Doyle. "I don't know how you did it. I don't know how you got past Stonehead. But this is it. This is where it ends." He didn't blink, he didn't draw breath. He just stared at Doyle.

Doyle reached into his pocket. Wood's arm, the one holding the gun, stiffened, and he thrust it purposefully toward Doyle. Slowly, Doyle pulled out a packet of tissues. He ripped the pack open with his teeth and rolled them around his fingers in an effort to stem the flow of blood. Wood took a step forward. "You're a hard bastard to put down Doyle. I'll give you that."

Doyle patted his pockets as if he were looking for more tissues then reached across with his left hand to his right pocket. The blood had already seeped through the thin layers of paper and was dripping on the floor.

Wood puffed out his chest, thrust up his chin. "But I'm harder. I'm the Man, I'm…"

Doyle drew, cocked, and fired the .38 as he pulled it from his pocket.

Wood felt a solid thud and stopped speaking. He stared at the circle of red on his chest. He stared as if it were the strangest thing he had ever seen. The shot came from nowhere. Wood looked up at Doyle, his eyes questioning, saw a short-barrelled pistol in his hand.

Doyle fired again. Using his left hand and the pistol's double action, Doyle's aim was off. It hit Wood in the abdomen. The next tore into his shoulder. Wood staggered. He sank to his knees and looked at the gun in his hand. Even now he tried to drag it round and point it at Doyle.

Doyle stepped forward and knocked the Berretta away. Cocking the .38 awkwardly with his left thumb, he pressed the barrel to Wood's forehead. Wood's eyes focused. He grimaced, tried to speak, declare his defiance. It was too late. Doyle squeezed the trigger.

Wood's head flew back. His body followed and slumped to the floor. He lay with his legs folded beneath him, head to one side, and didn't move.

Doyle took a deep breath and looked at April. She stood motionless behind the counter. She looked at him like he was some kind of monster. Maybe he was. Maybe he wasn't fit to keep company with normal, everyday human beings. Doyle looked into her eyes, looked deep for there was something he needed to know. Seconds passed. He had to ask. As he opened his mouth, he heard the distant wail of sirens. Maybe it was best not to know. Maybe he should let things be.

Doyle turned his back and walked away.

It was easy. He had done it once before.

8 – TWO WEEKS LATER

John Doyle folded his paper and looked out at the sea rolling over the shore. It was November and except for a few hardy souls walking the promenade, Brighton's sea-front was deserted. Doyle found a comfortable spot, a café sheltered from the wind where a miserly sun warmed his back.

The place also served a mean Italian coffee.

He had been there two weeks, telling Mrs. Carnegie, the landlady of The Seaview Guest House that he was recuperating after an accident at work. A hand swathed in bandages was proof enough of his status. He paid his bills, kept to himself, and didn't come home drunk. She left him alone, and that suited him.

Doyle sipped his black coffee, toying with the pack of cigarettes on the table, back to forty a day. He flipped the lid and teased one out with his teeth. In the same pocket as his lighter he found his phone. It was a cheap Nokia, picked up from the supermarket. It hadn't yet been used. He hadn't spoken to Josie for over a week, but it paid to be careful. It wasn't so easy to lose yourself anymore. Doyle reasoned it was time enough. His finger punched in Josie's number.

Her voice was hesitant. "Hello?"

"It's me."

"John. I thought..." She exhaled in relief. "Why haven't you phoned?"

"I have my reasons."

"I'm sure you have."

Doyle caught the thinly disguised irritation in her voice.

"Are you still in Brighton?"

"Yeah. You haven't told anyone?"

Josie hesitated. "Only April."

Doyle rolled his eyes. "I said no one."

"I know, I know. It's just..."

Doyle mentally saw her shrug her shoulders.

"Well, it's only April."

Doyle sighed. "Yeah, it's only April."

"You in a hotel or something?"

"Best if you don't know."

"I guess you're right. It's been murder here."

"Yeah?"

"The police have been here nearly every day."

"What have you told them?"

"Nothing."

Doyle nodded. "That's good Josie. You know nothing about me okay?"

"If that's what you want."

There was an awkward silence. It was strange, thought Doyle, two people who had shared their lives now had nothing to say to each other.

"How is April?"

"She's good." Josie sounded hesitant. "She's quiet. A little..." Doyle could almost see her scrunch up her face, the way she did when she tried to find the right word. "Moody," was what she eventually said.

"Where is she?"

"She's gone away for a few days. The coast with friends. I thought it would do her good. You know, after what happened."

"Nice."

"When are you coming home?"

"Not yet," he said. "I need to keep my head down a little longer. With Wood gone you don't know who will step into the vacuum. You understand?"

"Yeah."

There was another pause. "John," she said and he could hear her pushing the phone closer to her mouth. "You *are* coming home?"

He took a breath. "Sure," he said. "Just not yet."

"Okay, John."

Doyle nodded. "Give my love to April." He broke the connection, paused, and dropped it into the waste bin at his side.

His coffee was cold. For a moment he thought about ordering another, then glanced at his watch. Maybe not. His dinner would be on the table at five. If he wasn't there, then he didn't eat. He left a few coins on the table and started to walk back.

Mrs Carnegie was waiting for him in the hall and pounced before he had time to even close the door. "Mr. Doyle." Coming from behind the little counter that served as reception, she stood in front of him. It was a long hall with potted plants, and photographs of pre-war Brighton on the walls. To the right, a long flight of stairs spiralled up out of view. She was a small, neat woman with graying hair tied back in a bun. Always formal, always precise, but Doyle sensed a change to her normal constitution.

"Mr. Doyle," she said again, quieter this time. She rubbed her hands as if a plague of ants were walking over them. "You have visitors."

His belly crawled. Doyle didn't get visitors. No one came to see him.

"She said she's your daughter." Mrs. Carnegie shrugged an apology. "I saw no harm and let them in your room to wait."

Doyle frowned and felt Mrs. Carnegie's hand on his wrist.

"I did do the right thing didn't I? Her friend," and Mrs. Carnegie hesitated, "was quite insistent."

Upstairs a door opened. Doyle turned his head to look. Two figures stood at the head of the stairs. He squinted, moved his head side to side as he tried to see. "April?"

It was her. She seemed older and her hair was cropped shorter than he remembered. He forgot himself and smiled. The smile died on his lips. Lurking in the shadow of the stairwell was another woman. Small, ash-blond, Doyle had never seen her before, but as she stepped into the light there was something unmistakable in her look, her stance – the way she would have looked after pushing her shopping trolley into Josie at the co-op. Brenda Wood didn't speak nor even smile, but reached into her bag and a moment later Doyle found himself looking down the barrel of large caliber revolver.
A .44 magnum if he wasn't mistaken.

Mrs. Carnegie gasped and slid out of view, locking herself in the parlor. April melted into the darkness, and now it was just he and a woman whose husband and nephew he shot dead a few weeks before.

Doyle was aware of the world closing in around him. His senses picked out things that a

98

moment ago would have passed without a thought: the tick of the clock, the deep red weave of the stair carpet, and from the kitchen beside the hall, the smell of meat cooking in its own juices. He should say something, he really should. The muzzle of that .44 grew larger and larger until it seemed he might lose himself in its cavernous opening. He glanced behind him. The door was still open. Calculating the distance between himself and Brenda Wood, he wondered if he could make it.

Stick or twist?

Brenda Wood didn't give him an option. She took a step and then another. Slowly she descended the stairs. The gun was a cannon in her hand. Just him, her, and nowhere to run.

A thousand things whirled through his brain, Josie, Ireland, the people he left behind. For the first time, John Doyle felt life weigh heavily on his shoulders.

And at last he truly knew what it was to be a man alone.

Acknowledgements:

Many thanks to CJ Edwards and Chris Rhatigan at for their belief, support and hard work in seeing this project to fruition. I am forever in your debt. Eric Beetner for his incredible artwork. And to Ann, my personal soundboard and proofreader for putting up with me all these years.

David Siddall lives and writes in Liverpool. His work has appeared in various magazines and anthologies including: *Noir Nation*, *Heater*, *Mysterical-E*, *Supernatural Tales*, and *Dark Visions 2*. A man Alone is his first novella.

Printed in Great Britain
by Amazon